## About the cover artist

During his lifetime, Frank Terry was a soldier, inventor, artist and devoted husband and father. After World War II where he flew 45 missions as a radio gunner on B17's, he married his sweetheart Mary and they had two children Frank Jr. and Nancy. He worked his entire life supporting the family. In his later years he developed a keen interest in art in all its forms.

A self taught sculpture and painter, he loved nature and people. He painted numerous seascapes, forest settings and portraits. His works grace the walls of family, where they are held in high esteem and regard.

He is gone now but his works remind us all of his love of life and nature's beauty. (Written by Frank Jr.)
Edited by Lilly Iamson

## Dedicated to Frank Terry

# Alone

## By

## Lilly Iamson

Cover art by Frank Terry

Arrow pushed the bone of her ankle back into place and watched the skin heal over. This was the tenth time she hurt herself on purpose to watch it heal. No one else on the entire planet that she knew of could have possibly healed that quickly. Arrow dug a fingernail into her palm and watched the drops of blood vanish from her hand. "I hate to tell you this," a voice called from the mouth of the quarry, "But I can't climb down there."

"I'll get up, just a minute." She answered, pulling the leg of her pants down again and dusting off her hands. She climbed out of the crater towards Tib, who tapped his foot impatiently.

"Do you plan on telling me why you're always here?"

"I can't really give you an answer," she kicked a rock into the quarry causing a little musical crack as it danced to the bottom, "Why didn't you just go back to Westridge?"

"You said we could work together on those panels tonight. Rage said you came out here."

Damn her bunk mate always knowing where she'd be when she wanted to be alone. "Tibur, how can I help you right now, at six in the morning?" she said it calmly but he felt how unwelcome he was with the look she gave him.

"Shot to the head, I'm sorry to bother you," he dropped his shoulders and started to turn around.

"Come now, don't leave until you explain."

"Blade told me that you haven't been eating with the girls and she wasn't sure what was wrong." He pointed to a mesh bag of navel oranges on the ground, "I found a tree and since these are your favorite, I picked a few."

"Tibur," she felt terrible, "I haven't been hungry in a few days, but thank you."

"What are you doing here though?"

Arrow thought quickly, he wasn't a gossip and she knew she could trust him. "I think I may be more different than I even look."

He had no reason to argue that she was not like anyone he had ever met. Her skin was pale and her hair was lighter than any he'd seen before, "in what way?"

"Only if you swear never to tell anyone," Her blue eyes were fiercely intense.

"Who would I tell?"

"Swear," she said again more forcefully.

"Okay, I swear I will never tell another person whatever it is you want to share with me."

"Cut me," she handed him a knife from her side belt.

"Are you kidding?" All the blood in his thin cheeks had leaked out.

"I promise I'll be fine," she nodded an encouragement putting out her arm. He cut her and the sight of blood had him near closing his eyes, "Look." He watched it heal in a blur against his own beliefs.

"What does that…What are you?"

She felt the jab she was afraid would be everyone's first reaction, "Now you know why I'm not hungry." She snatched back her knife, "I'm still the same I ever was." She sulked sitting on a rock near the edge of the chasm.

"You aren't in any pain?" he stepped over taking the arm he cut into his dark hands and running his rough finger along the closed wound that he could no longer see.

"None physically," she shrugged.

"I'm sorry, that wasn't what I should have said."

"Can't blame you, I've felt like I grew a second head since I discovered my…anomaly."

"How about we call it your ability?" he suggested gently and she smiled nodding her agreement.

## Chapter 1

The world went dark; Arrow blinked her eyes and glanced towards the sky. A warning scrolled across the expanse above, 'The floor shakes all over, each town will have to save themselves and you can't help the one you stand beside.' She saw flashes of explosions and then it felt as if her body was being propelled to the next point of impact, at least a hundred times she was shot forward to one impact after another until she landed at home. The seventy-five acres of Westridge orphanage, the place they all lived, filling positions in the staff after they were simply too old to adopt or returned by a set of parents who didn't want them. When her sight cleared she was standing, untouched with no sign that anyone had any idea what had happened everywhere else. The televisions didn't come on during the daylight hours, so if anything had happened she'd have to wait until after dinner. She didn't remember leaving her room as she realized she stood in the grass outside, no one else was up and about yet so she crept back in to help the cook make breakfast.

"What are you doing up little Arrow?" The burly man had always called her little.

"Had a bad dream and I needed some air," he nodded in his all knowing way as he passed her the biscuit dough to roll out.

"I don't suppose you woke your shadow to tell him about it."

"No, Bow went to sleep too late, didn't seem fair."

"He'll be up for breakfast," he laughed, "Not much to do this morning so once you finish those biscuits, get on out of here." She agreed and spent a few minutes cutting trays of perfect squares until it was all gone. She put them in the oven and walked down the hall to the library where she dozed off against a wall with a book about the world in 2200 virtual reality and what it did to society. When she awoke it was time for lunch. Drowsy and thoughtful, she went down to the kitchen and ate before going to her room to write as much as she could think of to help her friends survive what she'd seen.

~~

"You don't understand Steel. I can't stay here and not tell people what I know."

"So you hand me a hundred pages and want me to blindly follow this plan?" she took his hand.

"Tib will help you and I've created a core group of people who have the skills you'll need to build the fort."

"There's a fort in here?" he glanced at the weighty packet wondering intently what all was included.

"Steel, the world is going to come to an end and not just as we know it."

"What does that mean, Arrow?" He insisted.

"Three quarters of the population of the planet is going to be wiped out."

"I still don't understand why you know this."

"If I tell you then you can't tell anyone exactly what I say, ever." Her piercing blue eyes wouldn't have let him lie if he tried.

"Alright, I swear never to share any part of this conversation if you swear to tell me exactly what you know."

She took a deep breath, trying to calm herself. "The world will be destroyed by explosions all over the planet at specific points of both military and technological bases. Tokyo and all of China will be gone and part of Russia. The US will lose nearly everything."

"I still don't understand how you know all of this."

"I think it was accidental." She tried to wave it off.

"Tell me exactly, you promised," Steel pressed.

"The whole thing came to me in a dream. I was moving from one site to the next and seeing all these places completely destroyed. It reminded me of the old nuclear videos about V-world and how they placed all those perfectly in line systems that made everything run smoothly. The vision was like a briefing given to a long dormant soldier awoken from hyper sleep." She left out that she was outside when she came to consciousness, afraid it would be too weird for him.

His face was blank of emotion, "Arrow, when did this happen?"

"Two nights ago," he pulled a knife from his pocket and took hold of her quickly giving her no time to react. The low table that had been between them hit the far wall breaking its top against the closet door frame. "What are you doing?" she screamed before he covered her mouth in a hand that nearly covered her entire face and sliced into her exposed thigh.

She fought her hardest to try to hide herself but he saw her heal back without so much as a scratch. "I'd have done that a long time ago but who can be sure?" he let her go where she fell to her knees on the floor. "Sorry to be so forceful but you wouldn't have shown me had I asked."

"How could I?" she stood up slowly, terrified that he would say something to someone else.

He sensed her feelings and held out his own hand cutting it with the same blade. He healed, faster she thought, "Whatever we are it's the same, but I didn't think of saving anyone when I had my dream."

"Why didn't I tell you about this?" She mused aloud.

"For the same reason I never told anyone, everyone wants to hurt or alienate any people who are different."

She thanked her lucky stars for Tib, "I suppose you're right. I still need these things to be done for our friends and our future."

"Can it work?"

"I don't want to get your hopes up but I believe so."

"And Tib doesn't want to be the leader in your absence?"

"Who would listen to him?" she smiled.

A few days later, Tib was stuffing money in as many places as he could in her backpack while she showered in the next room. Tomorrow she would be on a plane to the northwest to start giving as many people as she could a heads up about the destruction to come. He had no idea where she was going exactly but there was no way to stop her and she'd refused his company. All he had left was stuffing every cent he had into that bag to help her get back. The water stopped and he zipped it up, hopeful that she wouldn't notice anything until she was long gone. Over the fifteen years they'd known one another she never showed any kind of weakness or asked him for anything after the secret she shared at the quarry.

"Hey," she smiled, white blonde hair hanging wet down her back in the t-shirt and jeans she wore.

"Hey, the maintenance guy let me in to see you. I don't think he realized you'd be in the shower."

"No, I'm sure he didn't." she toweled her hair between her hands, "Are you trying to get your goodbye out of the way early?"

"Something like that." he stood from the bed next to her bag. "I still don't understand why you have to leave by yourself but I'll work with everyone else to do the best I can."

"Tib...I've never been good," he cut her off.

"I know. That's why I'm saying my goodbyes in private."

"You have more to say," she crossed her arms across her chest and Tib lowered his eyes.

"You should make sure you get back here with me."

"With you?" he nodded, "I'm listening."

"We've been avoiding one another since your vision and I hate it, when you come back I hope you'll be yourself with me again."

"It scared me to see all those things."

"I realize that, but I'm still myself no matter if you can protect me or not. I want to be sure that you'll come back."

## Chapter 2

Arrow was waiting for the general in a clean parlor room within the offices of an Army base. She'd gotten an appointment from a nice woman over the phone and was led in exactly on time by a man in full uniform and multiple shiny, dangling medals.

"Take a seat Ms. Arrow," she obeyed with her usual confidence. "My morning briefing said you had information you would only share with me personally."

"Yes sir," she glanced at the officer still standing by the door at full alert. "I do believe I asked to have a private conversation."

"Step out lieutenant Strobe." his heels snapped together saluting before ducking out. "Proceed."

"I have reason to believe the US may be under attack in the next seven to nine months."

His face betrayed no belief that she was onto anything, "How is it that you're in possession of this information and possibly more importantly, attack from whom?"

"Domestic threats sir, overlooked nuclear repeater stations buried in secret places, subterranean nuclear reactors created to power V-world breaking down and perfectly spaced across this great nation and the rest of the planet, sir."

He nodded thoughtfully, "Do you have any specific locations to perhaps move on preventative measures?"

"I don't think it's possible to back track this particular situation as it's been a decade or more in the making. What I do suggest is a safe place that people know about before anything happens, somewhere to travel to once the dust settles."

"That many people will be affected?"

"I have reason to believe that only a third of the world will survive the blasts and still fewer will survive the chaos afterwards." He responded with another thoughtful nod. "Sir, I'd like to ask a few of your men to head to that safe place I mentioned and report back to you." He paused, watching her in an uncomfortable silence.

"I'll send my lieutenant, he's got the same kind of inklings and perhaps your little 'safe place' will help settle him."

"I'm not the first person to tell you about this threat?"

He shook his head for a long time, "You're the first to give me a feasible enemy we wouldn't necessarily have the tools to defeat and you included more than 'us' in the warning." he sat back in the brown leather chair that creaked under his weight, "Does this place you spoke of need a military presence?"

"No sir, we only need to be tucked into the back of your mind. When the chaos has ended and few people are wandering, I want those people to have a direction to travel."

"So you're collecting the refugees to help 'us' bounce back as a society."

"For lack of a better word yes, refugees. I prefer to think of them as survivors. They'll be the strongest and possibly the smartest of our country that make it all the way then we have a chance to rebuild civilization with more focus on just that."

He hit a button on his desk top. "Come back Strobe." no one answered but a moment later the lieutenant entered again. "Tell him where to fly out to and how to get there. I suppose someone is there to greet and receive him?"

"Yes, my entire core of engineers and our leader, who I appointed before coming to meet you."

"Where am I going?" Strobe asked with concern. Arrow filled him in on exactly what he would be doing and she saw him relax. "It sounds perfect, outside of the city and surrounded by forest. Shouldn't be destroyed or easily found." he sounded giddy.

"You're to head there and report back here," the general spoke up. "Fill a file that I can leak to the public, I'm not saying this is happening yet but I'll send provisions as they become available for the people working on the physical structures."

"Thank you Sir, I'm sure Steel will send his thanks as well."

"Steel... sounds like a very strong leader." he mumbled as they were excused by a nicely dressed woman in horned rim glasses for his next appointment.

"You may well have saved my life ma'am," Strobe held out his hand to shake hers.

"Please, call me Arrow and once communication is lost be absolutely loyal to Steel. He'll be glad to have someone so highly recommended." She shook his hand curtly then strode out to find the four corners monument that Steel said was a must see.

As she sat in the center of the huge block marked off for the four states she thought about where she would be going next and how difficult it might be to talk to someone once she got to the one top secret base she knew of. The general of the last had been so kind and accommodating that she hardly had to do anything to get a meeting.

~~

Forging nails, Bow swiped some sweat from his brow, "Think we can finish this in time?" Steel shrugged his shoulders and dumped out the last five half cooled nails from the press.

"I don't know what's going to happen until I get to the next page each day. Bow poured the cast full again, snapping the top down with his poker before the pressure began to mash them hard into the mold.

"Shouldn't you read ahead?"

"No, that's why the captain holds onto the map."

"So, is this a treasure hunt then?" Steel slowly shook his head, loading the cooled nails into the bucket at his side. "Then it's some fort, like Pine said?"

"Yes, in a manner of speaking. I am following the plans for a seven foot tall walled community where we can all live in safety."

"But why custom make our nails and screws? I know they're bigger than average but there's got to be some place we could find them and skip the work."

"I'm using the materials Arrow sent us last week."

Bow looked over to the sheets of raw steel with a new appreciation. "Could I see the plan?"

"Each page is labeled and there's an index. You have three pages near the end and like I said before, I'm following the plan."

Bow was so confused, she hadn't said a word about her plan before she left, only asked him to work alongside Steel and help as best he could while she was gone. If he hadn't gone to her room, she wouldn't have even said goodbye. Later that night he sat down to a half filled piece of paper and wrote a second letter that would never be delivered.

(Arrow,

Steel says you left me instructions but they're at the end of your well organized packet or plan and I can't see them until we've completed the fort or whatever it is you drew up for us. I've been working like I promised but I'm exhausted where these guys never seem to tire. I'm stronger than I used to be, still nothing like Steel but stronger than before. I have a suspicion that he's like you but I'd never tell anyone your ability so I'll likely never know.

I keep wishing you'd never gone away in the first place. How am I to continue without my sweet Arrow to goad me on?)

~~

Years of crack pots trying to get a closer look led to thirty mile wide containment area and ten foot tall barbed wire fences another mile outside of them. She was ready to forget it until a pick-up truck pulled up behind her.

"We need you to leave," a bull horned man demanded.

"I'm not going anywhere until I speak to someone in charge." she yelled back.

"No one talks to reporters here, move along."

"I have no idea what gives you the idea that I'm a reporter."

The man stepped out of his truck, striding toward her almost as gracefully as she would have. "No one is admitted beyond that gate without an invitation or an appointment and you have neither."

"Says who?"

"I would have been told."

"What's your name soldier?" he was easily twice her girth in muscle but she thought it may be possible to outsmart him.

"Sergeant Timber, what is your name, not a reporter?"

"Arrow. No title or anything."

"What are you doing out here little projectile?"

"I need to warn your leader of the impending threat."

"A threat huh? Is it bigger than you, because if you're the threat it's been contained."

She knew he was right, she had nowhere to run and he had a gun and a truck. "It's far greater than me."

He scratched his head, "I've never seen anyone get past the gate without an invitation or orders, there's really nothing I can do."

"Then you tell them that in four months the world will change and I know of a place to go after the fallout." She handed him a map to Port and the basics of survival list she and Tib had written up together.

"You want me to give this to the General?" she nodded, "He'll discharge me as a loony."

"Then you go there." She pointed to Port harbor on the map.

"Sure lady, now move along." That was the best she could hope for and she was confident his officers would be told about this. One more place to go, one more person to convince to move towards safety. It was a mile before she noticed the sergeant had followed her, "Are you going back to this place?" he asked, hanging from the window of his pick-up truck.

"No." she kept walking with the truck keeping pace.

"Where are you headed?" she stopped.

"Aren't you going to give that to someone?"

"My superior was in my ear the whole time, he told me to follow the map and send back reports about what I see." Arrow recognized the pattern now, anyone exposed to her or the Port was used as a guinea pig.

"I have to get to the west coast, a marine base out there was supposed to be my last stop."

"Can I take you to the airport?" She was surprised by the offer and accepted instead of questioning. Neither of them was very talkative and she felt comfortable in his presence, he wished her safe travels at the airport ticket counter and went to buy a ticket for himself.

~~

Months later and books filled with letters to her had allowed Tibur the privilege of completing his portion of the packet. He chose the best animals to keep in Port which seemed foolishly useless to him. Goats, pigs and chickens were clearly useful but he wondered whether they would need cows and horses as well. Ultimately he chose to take in a few cows and he got three horses just to be safe. After he caged the last of the chickens into the finished pens, he turned to see Steel greeting a tall, broad man in uniform near the main gate on the west side of Port. He strode over to listen.

"...She said that things were already in motion here and I was simply to observe and report to my superiors of the safety and accommodations."

"I'll have Pine show you around and get you to and from a post office if you need that."

"Thank you sir," The man clicked his heels and saluted before following Pine through the mess hall where they all currently lived while barracks and out buildings were under construction.

"Who was that?"

"Soldier from Colorado, says Arrow gave him our coordinates and his commanding officer put her in a safe place for at least one night."

"Is he the first word we've gotten?"

"She is alive and doing just what she set out to do." He clapped Tib's shoulder.

"Of course she's alive. I never had a doubt about that. I just hope she'll be safe out there. This date is quickly approaching."

"Don't worry yourself until we've finished the packet completely." Bow nodded gravely, the end was still only a concept they were defending, he feared the day it became a reality.

~~

Detonation began the exact way she said it would and the core group sat in bed rolls ten stories underground in the mountains near Port. Crate, Silver, Pine, Blade, Strobe (the soldier), Bow, Willow and their newest arrival Timber; listened as hard as they could for the ground to shake. Tib mouthed prayers for Arrow's safety and shut out his lantern. Willow was crying and Pine was trying her best to soothe her though she felt very disconnected herself. Strobe switched off his light next and disappeared into the dark like Bow hoped he had as the few tears he allowed to fall slid down his face. They planned to remain underground for at least a week but hardly made it six days before Steel needed to get some fresh air and natural light. The Port only sustained minor damage that were easily repaired within a couple of days and then the people began to arrive, people that were injured and scared. Tib couldn't stand it, the masses poured in with nothing to offer them and resources to use along with needs to fill. A square mile became a country, filling with a diverse mix of people who all wanted security again and some kind of normalcy. Tib resented them all for the sure way they answered their Port oaths.

On the day he was to take his position in the Core he gathered two duffel bags of canned foods and left with no intention of ever returning. It was foolish of him to think that he could belong there without her.

## Chapter 3

She had traveled seventeen hundred miles by foot, with little more than her laser gun and the liquid converter she pulled out of a burned out surplus store she stumbled upon in her first few days. Half crazed from dehydration she'd thought it was a mirage until she fell, tripping over the charred remains of the outer wall. She dug up as many things as she could and ended up with twenty packaged meals soldiers carried, a backpack and the converter.

Traveling light seemed the only logical way to go, avoiding the main highways and not taking anything she couldn't carry. The world was a dark place at night now that the lights had stopped coming on a full six months after detonation. Computer systems were working unmanned for at least that long but now she was outside the grid and it was terrifyingly dark and desolate.

She was creeping down a deserted country road that she didn't recognize, though it felt vaguely familiar. She assumed that her journey had taken her to the swamp lands but it made little difference as she hadn't seen another living person since she began. Stores were almost completely empty of non-perishable food items and she used her limited plant knowledge to get her this far. She kept hoping to come upon someone, anyone, so she could be sure she wasn't alone on the planet. Home wasn't gone, she comforted herself, her friends were strong and smart and the chaos was not too much for them to overcome.

Seven months she walked, hoping that somehow they were the ones who survived all the explosions the way she'd seen. She hoped that all of it happened in bigger cities with more old buildings not anywhere near home. They were a port city with very few of their own products or exports and not a place with any metals worth digging up along with only one teleportation transit station nearby. Yes, they were all fine, no doubt.

The wind changed direction and Arrow could smell smoke, clean smoke, like someone had built a fire instead of the jumbled smells of the forest itself burning. She hunched down, glancing under the tree cover and over the grass. It looked like a bonfire, could it be? Abandoning the careful way she had traveled thus far she left the road walking directly to the expertly placed pyre. Stunned, Arrow stared at the licking flames without wondering who built it.

"Hey you!" She flinched and drew her laser gun.

At first, frantic glance she saw no one in any direction and said nothing. Aiming the gun in the direction she heard the voice, "Show yourself."

"You have a gun. I'll stick to my hiding place." It wasn't a stupid person at least, Arrow thought to herself as she put the gun back into her waistband.

"Better?"

"Not really, I saw you draw that thing before," her eyes found him in the trees ahead of her, "Mind if I ask your name, everyone I've met along the road was looking for someone."

"You've seen others?" she sat on the ground by his blazing fire, shocked to have found anyone else in the world.

He nodded slowly, "Do you have a name then?"

"Arrow, I lived in the west when the bombs started." He hopped down from his perch, still timid for her obvious skills with the weapon.

"I can say with all honesty that no one asked for you." He gave her a crooked grin.

"Of course not, I'm the first person you've seen in months too." She plucked a few blades of grass before he nodded the truth.

"I thought there was a bear coming to eat me, so I climbed the tree." He was being more social than she felt and the whole thing was silly to her suddenly.

"A bear could have gotten to you down there," she pointed out. "The low branches aren't really safe enough."

"Yeah but you were really fast, I barely lit that and you were here," he tossed a few small twigs he'd accidently pulled trying to get out of the tree, into the fire.

"Proves we're both too comfortable in the open, what's your name?"

"I've forgotten my given name but I would answer to Flint, if you don't mind."

"Not at all, how old are you?"

"I guess I'm twenty now, how about you?"

"Twenty-five, I'm heading for the sticks. Do you have any plans to find family or friends?"

"Aren't any to find," he rubbed the back of his neck thoughtfully, "what's in the sticks?"

"My friends are down there." He sat next to her on the ground, looked into her clear blue eyes and scoffed.

"How can you be sure they survived?" she reached for the gun again, "alright, they're fine." He conceded without her pulling it from her holster, "I'm sorry."

She turned away, "You can join me if you need to but you have to pull your own weight."

"Alright," she was a great example of stoic calm. He knew immediately she would keep him safe.

"Will your friends be as agile and healthy as you are maybe with food?" she looked back at him and saw how very thin he looked. The obviously former healthy boy had withered in this desolation.

"How long has it been since you had a decent meal?"

"Define decent?" he chuckled, "At least a month, maybe longer."

"I'd be happy to find you something to eat," she dug into her bag, "why the fire with nothing to cook?"

"I dropped and burned the two lizards I caught." He looked embarrassed.

"I have one foil meal left, Jambalaya?" She pulled the pouch from her backpack and set it on a rock, "Let's heat up some water and you can eat." This was just what she needed, another mouth to feed, but if he was the only other survivor they should travel together. He ate like he hadn't in months and she couldn't help but wonder how much longer he would have survived on his own. "I planned on getting another couple of miles tonight, can you do that?" He seemed healthy enough despite the boney appearance.

"Sure, I still don't know what you expect to find," he dug a hole and buried the empty package. "Can I get my pack?" she nodded and watched him rush off into the woods. In a few minutes he was back with a ragged duffel bag. "I have a couple of knives and this silver block I found."

He pulled out the two inch cube and handed it to her, "It's a light pod." She touched two sides and at once the whole thing lit up like a bulb without a switch.

"Wow, I wandered in the dark for no reason," he huffed, crossing his arms at his chest.

"They weren't common knowledge yet, this is what my friend Silver was working on." She tossed it back to him and watched him scramble to catch it. "Where'd you find it?"

"Some specialty shop is Seattle. Will the battery die?"

"There's no battery, it's powered by your body heat. Long as you hold it, it stays on." They walked for a long time in silence as Flint thought of the hundred ways his travels could have led in different directions and how lucky he was to have been found by someone like Arrow.

She started to feel pretty tired and looked up to see where the moon was, it looked like it was about ten, "You take first watch and wake me around midnight okay?"

"What am I watching for?"

"Large animals, people creeping up or anything that could potentially harm us." He nodded and started to scan the surroundings every few minutes. Flint hardly knew what kind of signs he was looking for but when nothing new turned up after a long time Arrow fell asleep and the next thing she remembered was being shaken awake.

"I think it's midnight." The moon was heading to the west, she guessed it was closer to two in the morning and took the chance to teach him the positions.

"I'll wake you at six," he sat himself against a tree and closed his eyes. She shuffled up a close by tree and watched from the low branches. She realized then that she felt a lot safer knowing she wasn't alone. Port still felt so far off but she had a companion now who actually needed her help as much as she needed the company. At the break of dawn she spied a rabbit climbing out of his burrow. She pulled her weapon, set to stun and took the shot, humanely killing it before she climbed down to retrieve their breakfast. "Hey, I got food. We have to get some miles behind us today. Two people can be followed a lot easier than one."

"Why would someone follow us?"

"Not necessarily someone, bears and wolves follow scents to find their food, how have you made it this far?"

"I don't know, luck I guess." she couldn't argue, he was very lucky to not have any missing body parts.

"You lit fires and slept in the open but you never thought about wild animals?"

"I didn't see any," He must crash around like a bigger animal, she thought.

"Well that's luck but now that we've doubled up the trouble is our smell." he sniffed his old worn out shirt. "It's like bacon to the carnivores."

"Oh man, I miss bacon." she nodded and smiled. They ate talking about their lives before detonation changed everything, Flint covered up the fire so they could leave without lighting the woods then helped her pack up to move on.

The next night was hot so she wanted to stop earlier than she usually would have. With no food there wasn't a reason to light up a campfire so they found a cool place to sleep and Flint lay down with her taking first watch. Half her watch had passed when he spoke up.

"If this is halfway, why isn't there any sign of this place?"

"I guess Steel didn't want to lead on that people were traveling the right direction. A bit of doubt so if they weren't sure it was the right way they wouldn't be until they arrived."

"Tell me a little about him."

"Okay..." she closed her eyes a second to picture him, something she rarely did so she always came up with his exact face in her mind. "He's tall with brown hair and eyes that look golden in the sun."

"How tall is tall?"

"Middle six feet, maybe six foot seven,"

"Oh, a giant?" she smiled wryly.

"A gentle giant, he's a little suspicious of people at first and if you cross him the cuteness falls away from his huge body and he kills you." Flint flinched and she laughed.

"I take it you two were close?"

"Best of friends, he's hard to push to that point really just watch what you say."

"I can do that."

The next day she knew they were closer than ever, when the sun went down she didn't stop or look for a safe place. "Are we bedding down tonight?"

"No, we're almost there."

They reached her home town in the middle of the night and there were twelve foot walls all the way around it, her smile made Flint uncomfortable.

"What is this place?" He asked in both amazement and a bit of fear.

"This is Port Harbor. My friends must have thought these would be hard to get over as a wild animal or starving traveler." She was inspecting them with her eyes and he couldn't help but worry they'd be exclusive.

"And they would let you in?"

"They should let us in, I can't abandon you after all this time," she made a move towards the path and tripped an ankle snare that she narrowly escaped. "If we aren't both captured before we get in." she joked feeling exhilarated by the near miss. Flint moved slower following her through the brush.

"You're sure they'll know you?"

"HALT!" a voice projected from the top of the wall, "Who goes there and what is your business?"

"I am Arrow. This is my traveling companion, Flint."

"What is your business?" the now familiar voice repeated a second time.

"I've been on a mission abroad for a full two years and I still know your voice, Steel," She heard a shuffle.

"Step back and we'll open the gate."

It was hardly a port, Flint searched each inch that he could see for water, as the giant door swung on mammoth hinges. There were fruit barrels lining the outside of a building and vegetables on the other side. He noticed goats in a vast pen with pigs, stables that were further to the east within the walls that he now saw went for a mile along each direction. A large man stepped out from behind the door once it opened fully and Arrow nearly jumped for joy, running to him.

You made it all this way?" he asked, convinced she was an illusion.

"I did," She took his hand to shake but was tugged hard into a hug.

"You can't possibly have walked all the way from the far coast?" but he could tell she had. The sun had touched her cheeks too much and she was far too thin for his taste, he let her go. "Young Flint here kept you safe?"

"He's been easy company along the road, hard worker." She grinned, "He didn't believe you guys had made it. Who's here?"

"Crate, Silver, Pine, Strobe and Timber of course are all here but I still haven't found any trace of Bow," his name wasn't Bow but she knew who he meant.

"What about Blade and Willow?"

"Here as well, the entire core made it through."

"I should go find Bow." Steel took her arm commandingly.

"It's been fourteen months since detonation. You were the last I suspected to make it and the farthest away. You were impossibly close to the origin site, I'm amazed you're alive," She knew the significance of the words from him.

"So you want me to say he's dead and forget it?"

"No, I'm saying he's dead and changing the subject."

Flint spoke up, "Can we stay here or not?"

"Any friend of Arrow is welcome," a girl in clean clothes appeared out of a building nearby with water and sandwiches on homemade bread, Flint nearly collapsed after his first bite.

"How well stocked is everything?" Arrow went on with her strong outer shell built up so thick she couldn't accept the nicety without asking or being told.

Steel had known her through her school years and wouldn't let her turn it down while Flint was through a second sandwich but slowing down. He handed her a sandwich and took her arm leading her away to talk, "How did you manage to get here?"

"Determination, blind determination to make sure that everyone I cared for was as safe as I'd imagined." She took a small bite of the peanut butter and jelly.

"We are, for the most part, right where you left us," he saw her searching faces and gently took her hand, "Tibur really isn't here, I wish he were. The man can build but he hasn't shown up in months."

"That's why I'm worried he may be looking for me somewhere."

"Don't blame yourself. He lived very close to our crater." She closed her eyes, wishing she wasn't going to believe him.

"Alright, what can I do here?" The whole place was bustling though she suspected understaffed. He got her fed and assigned them a room together at Flint's request. He couldn't sleep here without her. The next day she was to begin helping plant the rice, he was asked to go to the information center to be caught up on the groups' ways and aim in continuing intelligent life after this huge catastrophe.

"Are they cultists Arrow? Is that what this is, my brain washing appointment?" he asked, flailing his arms and pacing the room

"No," she giggled, much more relaxed now though he could tell that it was a thin veil over the grief she felt for her whole journey being for nothing. "Everyone here is kind and creative, they're gentle science types with no technology to work with and so a clear plan is in order."

"So, I'm in? No, walk the plank or hot coals or anything?" He settled onto the end of his cot.

"You arrived with the leader's friend and that was enough, I've already established trust in you."

"Who are you?"

"I am a very good friend by the strictest and oldest rules."

"Thank you, for taking me with you, you didn't have to." She smiled, the unhappiest he'd ever seen her and closed her eyes falling asleep.

He remembered her talking about Bow only once while they traveled. He had asked her what she saw when she closed her eyes and thought of home.

"The first thing is always the orange and violet sunsets and the glittering of the sandstone quarry all caught up in the excitement. Then it's Tib, people teased him and called him Bow, you know like bow and arrow." She'd explained needlessly, "He had the darkest crop of curled hair in town and the most interesting olive skin, with his slate gray eyes stabbing out from beneath his thick dark brows." Flint could almost picture him for the detail she gave. He felt then that he owed her the best company he could be if only for the chance she was giving him.

He crept out of their room walking down to the mess hall for some fruit. Steel spotted him and watched, trying to gauge this newcomer's possibility of integrating. He made his way over to him with a warm smile, "Can I help you find anything?"

"Oh, no, I see the oranges from here, thank you." Flint wasn't used to people helping him with anything even before the world changed completely. Steel started to walk away but curiosity was creeping up on Flint with a vengeance, "Are you willing to answer a couple of questions?" he asked without turning.

"Just between us?" Steel checked.

"Unless she asks me flat out," Flint was honest and Steel liked that about him immediately.

Flint wanted to know where her best friend was last seen and if there was any way he could have gone west looking for her. Steel thought this was all pointless but answered as best he could. "You know you can't go looking for him without significant risk and most definite anger from Arrow?"

"You think she cares about me now?" Steel saw a helplessness in the young, lanky man's eyes. "Her mission is complete and here she is among friends."

"You're a friend too."

"I have to re-pay her sir. I have to try at least."

"What happened out there?"

"I was starving when she found me. Had no idea where I was going or if there was anyone else left. I wasn't even sure she was real at first." He said the last sheepishly, she'd looked like his mother but Flint didn't have a mother.

Steel waited, "Still, Tibur isn't out there looking for her. He's gone." Just what he needed a damn vigilante bent on searching the woods for ghosts, at least Arrow was still logical and more importantly, she knew that accepting admittance here meant she was to stay.

"Sir, I have taken no shelter here yet and I'd like to step back outside of the wall for one week. To look at the place he lived, maybe get her a souvenir if he's gone forever."

Stunned at his pure intentions, Steel granted his request and loaded him up with a map and provisions for seven days. It was his loyalty that Steel found honorable and thought that if he cared so much for her perhaps in time, he could help her through the loss as well. Steel sent his own laser gun with Flint and pointed him in the right direction while he made a mental list to keep her busy for the time in-between, being a hard working determined woman who wasn't likely to ask questions, he didn't worry.

<u>Chapter 4</u>

Sunrise woke her like an electric jolt, she looked around the room for Flint but he was gone. She suspected early meal or study for classes and felt relief at the simple need not to worry.

The rice fields took all day to plant one sprig of grass at a time, she took a short hot shower and ate at a table with her old friends, none of whom felt very talkative. Hard work, she guessed, was taking its toll on everyone. In the old world none of this would have occurred to any of them, food came from the cafeteria, they'd never had to work in the garden or on the farms. The thought amused her as she ate her biscuit and glanced around for Flint a tenth time.

She knew she wouldn't sleep unless she was sure he was safe.

Steel caught up with her outside of the mess hall, "Arrow do you have a moment?" She nodded, coming over, "I've given your young friend a job that will keep him busy for a few days. He said to tell you he'd be fine." He saw her muscles relax.

"Good, I was worried for him."

"Is he as good a person as he seems?" Steel had needed to ask since he'd opened the side gate of the wall and let him out in the early hours of that morning.

"Better, he's very keen and loyal. I'm not surprised you found a use for him." She let a whisper of a smile play across her lips without noticing it herself. "He reminds me of Tib," The smile was gone as quickly as it appeared and storm clouds filled her already dark eyes.

"I am sure he doesn't mean to," she looked up to his smiling face, "He truly cares about you."

"Yes, he does, foolish boy," she smiled walking on to her room, Flint was enveloped into the fold, with a touch of loneliness she was proud of the character he showed. Outside the window she watched familiar faces pass by on their ways to bed or duties after dark, to which she imagined there were plenty. Pine had mentioned a few different 'after dark' safety precautions she thought were pointless when hardly anyone was wandering anymore. Arrow could see her point but knew that if no one had been on watch, Flint and Arrow would have been outside all night long.

She wanted to see him now, ask how he was fitting in and tell him what she'd learned about farming that day. She flipped off the lantern and shuffled down the cot under the potato sack blanket, tomorrow was a new day...

~~

Flint bedded down on the floor of Tibur's abandoned cottage, it had only taken him five hours to walk there and he'd tucked two pictures and a couple of notebooks into his pack. There were at least three other buildings nearby so he wasn't through looking just yet. His thoughts went to Arrow who was probably angry with him for just disappearing. He'd make it up to her soon he told himself.

Flint would never admit he'd lost an hour after he arrived, just staring at an old photo of her and Bow. Her eyes were shifted towards him with a bright smile that only the freest of carefree could pull off as they ran through a blurring field of white flowers. Flint imagined Bow looked so serious because he carried the camera and hated being the subject as much as he loved taking pictures of her.

The whole place was littered in paper and photos. He imagined the mad dash that left it this way and wished he couldn't, from the looks of it, hell froze over just about instantly here and the resident had very little time to fret about. There was something else bugging him though, no dust had settled on the useless appliances and the place didn't feel like it was empty all the time, it was unsettling.

He touched the sides of his light cube and spent a little more time memorizing the smile on her face in the candid photograph until he fell asleep…

~~

She woke to dark skies and the patter of fat raindrops on the tin roof, she grinned and stretched out. Then pulled on the gray long sleeve shirt Steel had put into the closet to get it up to standards. Everyone had the same crop of clothes, only what was needed and she loved the simplicity of it just being there, she wondered absently who did laundry around there and where.

Each person had a job and if ever you got tired of your job you could find another, again simple. Today she was helping in mess, peeling potatoes or chopping onions she supposed but it was likely under cover so she was happy to do it. Flint had been busy for five days and hadn't shown up once to check on her which felt strange though she wanted him to flourish and even pull away, but she always hoped they'd stay close like on the road.

Crate and Timber were moving boxes around in the kitchen when she got there twenty minutes early. "You are alive," she nodded to Crate with a subtle smile, "We'd hoped as much but Pine was sure you were dead." He chuckled.

"Not I," she replied without humor, "How about you and Pine, plan on tying the knot?"

"No such thing in Steel Town," Timber laughed stacking another plastic box of bananas.

"Excuse me,"

Crate continued, "No marriage, no kids and no way we could even live together. Steel is adamant that in time the rules will relax but until then separate quarters for all."

He'd let her have the room with Flint, or had he? "So Casanova here has to pine for Pine from afar," Timber punned.

"That seems for the best at the current time if you ask me. Are we company to any doctors?" Crate shook his head, he hated that she agreed with 'dictator Steel' but understood as well. The work kept the three of them busy until lunch was served and they took a break before dinner prep. Crate told her that two hundred and fifty people lived in the compound, a third of which were elderly or injured, everyone had a task if they were capable and he ran down the lists.

"Timber and I do food prep and the first part of most night watches, Pine has been helping Steel with all the questions people seem to keep coming up with. I think the best job here is Strobe's, he's been building hoses and couplings and horse shoes all from memory. Then Blade and Willow make paper and lots of plans for homes outside of the walls when things seem safer. We cut wood and plant crops thanks to all the help of Silver and her horticulture knowledge so we don't deforest too much of what's around us, just what we need."

The whole place ran without much need for Steel's leadership but he was an incredibly affective figure head to them all. In the first few months post-detonation crowds arrived in need of refuge and Steel had sorted them out or sent them on, if they didn't want to stay, in that he gained each man's trust and respect leaving his town unquestionably his. Those who came back never left again and he gave them a purpose. There was no iron fist, he led them to be commonly decent; take, then give back and expect those around you to do the same. His only other rule was everyone must contribute to stay and it was working out lovely. When all the work was done she showered and went to find Steel, which proved a simple task. He was stacking firewood in the square for everyone who needed it that night. She watched, noticing how muscular he was under the heavy jacket he seemed to wear all the time. He caught sight of her watching and looking vaguely amused at what she saw, so he waved finishing before jogging over. "Did you need me over here or are you just entertaining yourself with my toil?" he swiped some sweat from his brow absently.

"Did you send Flint away? I saw nearly everyone who works and lives here today through the window in mess and he wasn't there." His eyes were emotionless and steady, as always.

"I swear to you, I did not do that."

"Where is he?" he saw the flicker of panic you would from a mother who'd just found out her child was missing.

"Outside," he answered still steady and calculated, "He's been on a personal mission of his own request and design."

She was visibly shaken now and he was terrible with emotions on anyone but her wide eyes and quickened breath were obvious. "Flint left," she stated instead of questioned, she knew he couldn't lie any better than he could walk on water.

"I expect him back in two days."

"What is he doing?" she sunk down onto the grass under the tree.

"I couldn't begin to imagine what he's doing out there. He was starting at the ridge." Recognition of the place, then sadness, he knew Arrow's face so well, "He'll be fine. I gave him a gun."

"Might as well have given it to a kitten for its use to him, he can't shoot the broad side of a barn on full horizontal gaze," she was distraught, more than she had been for Bow and he was at a loss for words. No one had come to him for comfort and for good reason, he was not in tune to this. An orphan from birth, the only friends he had were orphans who cycled in and out of his life until detonation drove them back to the homestead where he waited warmly to greet them.

"Arrow, he will be okay these places are empty and I've been to them myself, safely." It was significant since she knew he was a coward under the surface.

"And when he comes back will he know you told me he was working, busily fitting in?"

"Only what you tell him, need he know," he helped her back to her feet.

"I know you've answered me already…" he cut her off.

"No sign at all, negative or positive, that he is anywhere alive. Arrow, I personally looked."

"I trust you, I just hope that no sign is positive." She smiled, gave him a brief hug and went back to her pitilessly empty room still with two beds even though one was always empty. Feeling bitter wasn't something Arrow was familiar with but Flint leaving without saying a word was hurtful, she kicked his cot. Still angry, she folded the wooden and canvas cot and set it on the other side of the room before getting into her own.

Steel had regarded them as friends until he watched her blue eyes go wild with panic at the news. Now he was sure it wasn't romantic as much as maternal, she'd stumbled upon an injured bird and nursed it back to health while finding it a safe place to live. Flint was being a good, thankful child in repaying her with all he could think to try. The whole thing warmed his heart and worried him that the injured bird may be hurt or lost again...

## Chapter 5

Back at the empty cabin, Flint sat in the open door drinking water and staring at that easy smile, when a stray page tried to escape the messy place. He caught it a few steps off of the porch and started to carry it back when he noticed it was addressed to Arrow. A flash of guilt was shrugged away as he read it.

(Arrow, The world is getting a little shaky around the edges and it's been less than a year since your plan went into effect. Op. Port Harbor is well underway and, as you expected, Steel is the perfect leader. I wish I knew you would get this or that you would care how it's going, from me, but Rage once said writing was a suitable way to get this stuff out of my head. I know I'm not the most handsome guy like Timber or the smartest like Steel, but I am the most trustworthy. I still haven't told anyone about your ability and I never would. When you get back, I'll be waiting to greet you and see if you've cooled to me or not, but until then I wait and work for you alone.)

The word 'alone', rung to him of the truest sadness Flint had ever felt. The note was outdated, even obsolete but he tucked it into a book in his pack anyway. Tomorrow he would head back to the Port, defeated in his mission to find Bow. He'd bring her the pieces he collected and let her yell at him for running off without telling her where he would be, then he'd try to blend into the community and do his part there.

A bush near the porch rustled and Flint knew it wasn't the wind. He reached to the gun at his hip and pointed it, as best he could tell, at the bush. "Show yourself," he demanded the way Arrow had when they met months ago.

"Whoa, lower the weapon there cowboy, some way for a man to be greeted at his own home." The dark man stood up and crossed his arms across his chest. "You still plan on shooting me?"

Flint was in shock, it was Bow most definitely, with the addition of an unkempt beard and a few less pounds. He lowered the gun slowly setting it to his left.

"Thanks," Tib took the five long steps to the stairs where he sat, "Name's Tibur," he held out his hand confidently shaking Flint's.

"Flint, why aren't you inside the Port?"

"I return your question with an addition, why are you here instead of there since you obviously know about it?"

He chewed his lip, not ready to trust him, "Doing a perimeter sweep."

"I'm waiting for a friend." He replied joylessly looking out into the fields of dying grass around his cabin.

"What's their name, people told me their names as they fled months ago."

"Her name is Arrow."

Flint nodded, knowingly, "I've heard about her, she was out west pre-detonation, right?" Tib nodded, sure that this guy knew nothing about her.

"Some point, she will get here and since I can't keep hiding from Steel, can you take back a message for me?" Flint agreed, without any further elaborating. "Tell him, Arrow is not dead no matter how close to the first site she was," He paused, "and as soon as she finds me we will both make it there."

Flint nodded, "Can I still stay the night?"

"Sure," Tib welcomed him in and fed him red meat like he was company. Flint was at a complete loss, did he tell this wild man where to find Arrow, (his Arrow?) or just take back the tokens he'd collected and tell her nothing then watch her live the rest of her life in sadness? He wouldn't dream of it but what to do? "Do you have any family still living?"

Flint was startled out of his own mind, "Not really, I traveled here alone until my friend found me she's all the family I have now I guess."

"Is she young like you?"

"Few years older but far healthier, she's like a sister and a mom in one."

"Sounds just like Arrow, except her and I are the same age." He shrugged, "I'm a broken record, feel free to talk over me," he thought he saw boredom on Flint's face but it was his guilt upsetting his stomach.

"Did you love her?"

"I do still, why else would I live alone in the wilderness without hope of ever seeing her again?" the question was rhetorical.

"You would never abandon her or change your mind about how you felt?"

"Never," he answered in a daze until his mind caught up to how confusing that question sounded from a stranger. "What do you care?"

Flint swallowed the knot in his throat in two gulps, "I know Arrow." He hadn't said knew, no, he said that right at this moment he was aware of someone named Arrow at the least. Tibur sat on the floor, stunned by the words and a bit incredulous. "She's at Port, waiting for me to get back." Still Tib said nothing, "We traveled in together," he continued.

"She is at Port now?" he nearly whispered the question.

"Yes, if I bring you back with me I may get a good head start at paying her back for saving my life." He waited a second, then another, "You are Bow aren't you?"

"No one's called me that since she left," he was beginning to think it was all in his imagination. He scooped up an armful of the scattered pages in the room then spoke to

Flint without looking at him, "I'll go back with you in the morning," standing, nearly completely hidden in the wild pile of papers, "Sleep well." With that he strolled into the bedroom in the back and closed the door. Flint made up his bed and lay there a long time staring at the ceiling, half congratulating himself and half wondering why Steel would say he was dead when he knew Tib lived. In the morning, he and the wild man would be starting back to safety and that soothed him to sleep since he didn't want Tib to see him with the photo…

~~

Arrow stood digging holes for trees of what would be an orchard, once they were finished. It was just outside East wall and she enjoyed the feeling of being freer than she felt inside. The wind was picking up and the dirt started to blow around, she turned to pick up her bucket of water to saturate the earth and saw Flint's unmistakable gait from a hundred yards. She dropped the handle to the bucket's side, shielding her eyes from the sun with a hand and noticed a second figure at his side, Tibur. Before her mind had even registered what she was doing she was in full run easily closing the distance.

Tib stopped, waiting for her to crash into him but she slowed a step away and stopped right within the circle of his arms. "Are you real?" after two years he couldn't trust his own eyes or even his sense of touch.

"Are you?" she replied.

Flint rolled his eyes, "You both are." She let go of Bow and pulled Flint to her with all her force.

"Thank you," was all she said, all she had to say. She walked back to Port between them, happy again though she hadn't allowed herself to notice how unhappy she had been. Tib had very little to say so Arrow told him about her journey, things even Flint hadn't known, as she took them to Steel.

"Flint, my boy, you found the shadow man." Steel looked pleased, "We'll get you a shower and shave soon Bow," he grinned.

"That would be agreeable though I have gotten attached to the beard," he stroked it thoughtfully with his free hand, the other held Arrow's like a vise, afraid she would fade away if he let go.

"A few days to re-build your strength Bow and then I need you on my Builders the way only you can be." Tibur nodded an agreement, "Flint should work with you at first, if you don't fit the job we'll try again." Flint agreed and he turned his attention to Arrow. "We will need to have a short heart to heart soon. I'm willing whenever you have time for me."

"Tomorrow perhaps, I'd like to spend some time with Bow." She looked radiant, he noted, incredibly happy and finally alive again.

"See you then dear," the two of them walked away together back towards mess, for water and a place to sit. Neither noticed leaving Flint behind.

"There, I paid her back right?" he posed the question to no one but Steel was still standing there so he came up with his own answer.

"Though she still cares about you, he is her confidante and oldest friend and once they catch up she'll be looking to thank you." Steel clapped him on the shoulder, "He would have come here eventually but you did the right thing."

"Yeah," he knew she wasn't lost to him but now she'd fall in love and forget him completely. "Got any underground work for a skinny kid with mining experience?"

"Mining," Steel considered, "We'll see what we can do."

## Chapter 6

"You knew the plan Bow, why weren't you waiting and working here?" his eyes never left her face, she looked so different yet just the same.

"I didn't want to let Steel down with my constant distraction over you," he lowered his voice to a whisper then continued, "I knew it was just a matter of time before you got here and came to me."

"Sorry I didn't come personally."

"Speaking of, who is this Flint?" He glanced around, "and where?"

"He must have stayed behind with Steel," he gave her a look reminding her of the first question, "He's a young man with more heart than strength and I feel he may see me as a sort of mother hen."

"More brain then you let on as well," he reached over to take her hand between both of his, "I am still just happy to see you again no matter who enjoyed your company while I waited, even Steel," she smiled remembering how jealous Bow had once been over him.

"Would I have come so far for him?" He leaned in, stopping just short of her lips and kissed her chin. She rolled her eyes and took hold of his face kissing him, "I missed you, don't ever deviate from the plan again."

"Yes ma'am." They ate dinner with Pine, Crate and Timber. Arrow found herself looking for Flint to join them but they finished and he never showed up, she excused herself from the table and went to find him.

After half an hour of searching she went back to her room, "Thought you'd never think to look here," he grinned from her cot.

"I thought you might have shoved off again, since you don't care to tell me when you do." she snapped back at his smugness.

"Well, I haven't let you get angry yet, so I stuck around for my lecture." She sat next to him, deflated by his wind sweeping statement.

"Flint, I was worried about you never coming back." His arm went around her shoulder, brotherly and protective.

"I got you something out there."

"Yeah?" he got up and opened his bag, pulling out the picture he'd been entranced by and handed it over to her, "I never saw this one after he took it, thanks."

"Forgive me yet?"

"Long way from it, thank you for finding Tibur, he knows my whole life, but you don't have to pay me back. We met because we had to."

"I wasn't sure if we still needed one another."

"I suppose you don't really need me anymore but I'd still like to be friends," he hugged her, "What, you thought I was through with you now that we found my friends?"

"Sincerely I did." She gave him her sternest look. "I realize now, of course, that the whole thing was foolish and I need to apologize again."

"No you don't, just stick around, get to know people here and always talk to me whenever you can," she grinned.

"Deal," she almost sighed in relief, "I should get out of your and Tib's room." She grabbed his arm for dear life.

"No, no you have to stay here not him, no way."

He'd never seen fear in her eyes before, even when she pointed a laser gun wildly into the trees, "What's wrong?" he let her drag him to her side.

"We can't sleep in the same room, I can't sleep near him."

"You're a grown woman, I've slept near you."

"Very big difference, you aren't attracted to me."

"True, you are old," he teased and kissed her cheek, "Will he kill me if I stay here?"

"I'm sure he feels the same way," she shook the thought away.

"Ask him what he thinks, please."

"Do you happen to know where they took him?" he clutched her hand running his thumb over hers, as he led the way, then went on his own to find Steel about a new place to sleep.

"Bow?" he excused himself from their friends who promptly scattered.

"Have you made up?"

"He was just waiting to give me this." She handed him the picture, "Do you remember it?"

"I do," he held it a long time, looking at her smiling face and how the flowers used to grow in the field around his cabin, "She looks like a happy girl, wish she would come back." He handed her back the photo.

"Flint needed to get me something, to help me for saving his life, as he sees it, and this is what he found."

"Less than a day after that you changed all of our lives," she knew what happened, "then you broke my heart."

"Did Steel not fit the bill, did I not come back?"

"What took you so long?"

"I found a lead that led me to a detour that split off into two different dead ends. I was chasing what's wrong with me then I gave up and on my way I found Flint."

"Your new husband, of course," He spat back with sarcasm that almost made her cry but Arrow wasn't willing to show him what he'd done.

"Is that what you think?" she stood her ground with a fierce anger brewing in her gut.

"Steel says it's a mother bird thing," his fire had cooled off at her swelling eyes.

"I think you are incredibly insecure considering the circumstances." He pondered all her meanings before saying anything.

"Where do we stand, you and I?"

"Can't you see your own feet anymore, how long have you been out in the woods?" damn it, he thought, he took her cheek and kissed her softly, she cooled off little by little and realized that Flint saw already that Tib loved her, she was terrified to feel anything when she knew Steel was somewhere warning them. "Bow you have to stop, we aren't supposed to form bonds yet." She eased him away with a firm hand.

"What does that mean? I'm not allowed to kiss you ever, until Steel lifts his bans?"

"Not publicly at least, we aren't exceptions to his rules, we're more aware of them than anyone else and we have the burden of helping."

"Arrow, I know what we are supposed to be doing here." He stuck a hand in his curly mop, "Two years of just waiting and hoping you'd make it back. I knew you were alive," his slate gray eyes were sharp, holding her gaze as he dropped his hand and reached back to take hers. "The exceptions will start with us because I will marry you."

"Who are you kidding, we didn't want that when it was possible." She looked into his eyes, "You aren't anything like you were back then are you?"

He knew she was absolutely right, "I still love you, which may be the last similarity left." She wouldn't hear anymore, she let go of his hand with a flick not unlike a person in disgust.

"Love isn't real Tib, how can you ever say it to me?" she was so angry.

"Stop deflecting for ten seconds and listen." She huffed out a breath that made him want to smile but he held it back, hoping she wouldn't think he thought it was a joke.

"You have my least defensive attention," she looked back at him.

"I haven't had the benefit of miles to walk or my own survival to worry about and it's been six hundred and thirty days since I've worked with my hands. My entire life has been 'where is Arrow today?'"

"That's what you need then, a long walk."

"No," he took a testing step towards her, "I need to hear everything you saw and how you felt and to be filled in morning, noon and night for the rest of my life."

"Of course, just what every man wants, a droning woman with nothing better to do then talk." He chucked her chin playfully.

"Bite your tongue. I have plenty of ideas on how to fill the time."

Steel saw them there all cozy and knew he'd have to tell his oldest friends that relationships weren't allowed in Port. "Hey guys," he interrupted.

"Timber already told me the rules. I'll fill him in if he'd just…" Tib cut her off with a kiss that stole her breath.

"As far as I care Tib, you can get back to your hut, but Arrow is willing to abide so make your choice. I won't allow anyone to break the law."

"You idiot," Steel was stunned into silence, "We aren't planning on going that far, don't worry your hair from your scalp on our account but I will kiss her and hold her hand because she is mine."

"Keep it behind closed doors and clean Bow," he nodded to her and walked away. She excused herself and followed Steel, "Can I help you?"

"That's why I have a two bed room, you knew he wasn't dead?"

"I'd hoped he was. I did that mostly because of Flint seeming overwhelmed when we even just walked away that moment and he needed you. He finds himself in your debt."

"I know, but your laws?"

"Tib is the grand inquisitor when it comes to questioning authority, swore me in himself you know then strolled out with provisions he didn't ask for and never came back," he shrugged, "I really did hope he was dead."

"So we are to be together against the law?"

He touched a gentle hand to her cheek, "Pine asked the same question and then let it go and Crate still loves her."

"I'm so confused."

"If it feels right, my words mean nothing and if it doesn't then you can call it law and feel better about saying no." she understood and he went on his way.

She wasn't ready for anything like what Tib was suggesting, she wasn't ready to be a wife in this fallout, and she refused to be that girl, the one who needed a romantic partner for every step of their life.

"So Tib was led to mess by Flint," Pine glared, "Steel told you the rules and you have two boyfriends anyway."

"Steel told you the same rules and you drag Crate around like you don't care at all," she retorted already filled with confusion and bitterness.

"I'm willing to wait so I don't undermine our leader who has good reasons, Arrow."

"I care for both of them but neither in the way you think, they're my Port Harbor without the walls."

"Are you saying what I think?"

"I don't pretend to know what you think, Pine."

"Wait," she looked into Arrow's eyes, "They're your family?" she not so much asked as accused.

"Impossible, I'm an orphan. No real family or fake but they are my safety net."

"You love them?"

"Why do you look so surprised?"

"Rage told me once that if you ever said that word, I should hit you really hard in the head to jog your memory."

"Her name always was the most spot on."

"Well, brace yourself," her hand went back.

"I love them, can't say it to either one but I do," she smiled.

"Fine," Pine let her hand drop, "I love Crate too but I want this place to work."

"I'll do my part," Tib was marching towards her and Pine walked away, "Had a man-to-man?"

"Yes in a manner of speaking," he pulled her in for a hug, "Flint told me about the bear in the forest."

"We weren't supposed to tell that story but maybe he just didn't want me to start turning it into a big fish story."

"You have to tell me how it tasted." His respect for her was completely renewed, "Arrow killed a bear… It sounds possible as strong as you are."

"Flint gave the final blow, we just wanted to scare it off but he was as hungry as we were." He pressed her for the rest of the evening for details then all night in the room with Flint. The three being together was necessary for Steel, he preferred the crowd to the company and Arrow had agreed immediately.

## Chapter 7

They each crawled into a cot and Arrow flipped off the light, she couldn't sleep here between the guys. Her skin was itching and she hated feeling so uncomfortable with two people who cared about her. Just when Flint's snores started to fill the room, she heard a shuffle from the other side.

"Can I get in with you?" Tib whispered to her and she moved letting him climb in behind her. His arm went fluidly around her waist, his chin gently tucked into her shoulder.

"This is nice," she whispered.

"I knew I was supposed to be here, exactly where I am."

"Tib?"

"Yes?"

"When we were talking today you scared me, I need to follow the plan down to the letter and that means we can't be bonded yet and we can't sleep together."

"I don't mind, really but I would like to hold you through every hour of every sleeping moment we share." He kissed her neck and cuddled close when she sighed.

"You'll be content?"

"I will be counting the hours until we have more. The moment we start I'll tell you just how many have passed." She fell asleep, comfortable for the first time in as long as she could remember and dreamt a sweet dream.

Steel inspected the west wall with Timber and Strobe then ordered ten more tall trees to be cut down before taking his lunch break. Flint was making rope outside of mess, obviously very far along his own train of thought. Steel dropped down next to him, "Where's Arrow?"

"She went with that no-account Bow, off doing who knows what outside of East gate." He was sulking and Steel just nodded his understanding.

"I had her first you know, so if anyone should be jealous let's start with me."

"Why don't you stop them? Aren't you worried they'll be doing things?"

He shook his head, "Nope."

"But your baby ban?"

"It's not real," Flint looked genuinely confused and Steel couldn't help but laugh, "I just want people to be serious about it when they do. Did Arrow tell you about her parents?"

"No, I assumed she lost them in the blast."

"They died of old age when she was sixteen and eighteen but she never cried she just planned the funerals and moved on. Then her bunk mate died in a freak accident and she did the same. When I told her about Bow, she was actually affected, I thought she'd cry but no. She really is happy now that he's back so I don't feel guilty for lying."

"I still don't follow."

"Bow was the last person that mattered in her life no matter how bad it was she had him but that wasn't the case the moment she met you."

"She won't ever cry if she has us both?"

"No, she won't get married or have a baby until I okay it because she has two of you already."

"What?"

"Just trust me Flint, she would never endanger either of you and she feels that becoming a mother would kill her."

"But she's so strong."

"It's how she became an orphan the first time."

"Oh," he said thoughtfully, "How did you have her first though?"

"She and I shared a room every day that she was in the orphanage and I stole a kiss once," he chuckled standing up and dusting off his clothes.

"Wouldn't she be crushed if something happened to you?"

"I'm likely to live forever," the gleam in Steel's eye had Flint agreeing, "Let's eat and then we can get some work done before lights out."

~~

"Why does Steel believe he'll live forever?"

"Three months and he's already buddy, buddy with big brother?" Crate scoffed.

"He has a secret. No one knows where he came from, him or Arrow actually," Pine answered.

"He knows where she came from though?"

"I suspect from the same place," Crate laughed thinking he was funny.

"So why is she so in love with Tibur if Steel knows her so well?"

Pine stopped Crate before he said anything else stupid, "Steel wouldn't talk to her once she got adopted not until the parents were both dead and Tib always paid her very special attention. One day they came back from her quarry holding hands and the rest is historical mystery." She bit into her apple to punctuate.

"Are you trying to say you have feelings for Arrow?" Crate asked seriously.

"Sure, I'm crazy about her," he rolled his eyes and left the table.

"That wasn't nice, he's younger than he acts and Arrow has been protecting him, he probably loves her very much." Timber hadn't said anything yet and took the chance to speak up.

"The whole lot of Arrow admirers, confuse and annoy me. She's just a girl."

"And if someone said that to you about me?" Pine spoke up to Crate's bitterness

"I'd kill them because you're my soul-mate."

"That's how each of them feels for her." He nodded finally feeling foolish for all he'd said.

### Chapter 8

Port was full of excitement that December morning, people moving cots to communal rooms and sleeping like big camping groups outside. The commingling was something most people missed. Feeling like you could flirt with one another and it wasn't completely fruitless at the end of the day. Some of the people who had arrived as couples were reconnecting but not everyone was thrilled with the rules change.

Arrow had to consider her entire life then and decide what she really wanted before she hurt both of the most important people in her life. She couldn't consult with anyone about it or even bring it up to Pine but she desperately needed someone's help.

'Where's Flint?' she wondered looking over the heads of people in the line at Mess. He was spearheading the community extensions, and since he'd met Blade outside on a chore he hadn't been sitting with her group. Arrow didn't mind him hanging out with new people, even Blade, but now it was hard to find him.

"Having trouble choosing a meal Arrow?" Steel filled his own tray with corn bread, rice and some beef stew from the recent slaughter.

"A bit distracted is all," she said through gritted teeth. He just smiled continuing on to a table, she slammed an apple and two bowls she didn't inspect onto her tray and stalked over to the table with him, "Are you proud of yourself now?" she wasn't loud or particularly angry sounding but her eyes told a different story.

"I really am, people are all a twitter with the changes," he smiled smugly with his spoon in hand.

"Wasn't thirty seconds after he read the proclamation that he said ours must be the first bonding ceremony in Port." Now she was almost sulking with the weight of it.

"You aren't even of this world, why are you so worried?"

"Because he is, how can I explain why we wouldn't be able to do the same ceremony as everyone else?"

"I'm listening," He kept eating like he didn't really care about the conversation.

"Am I shorting him of the true experience of bonding because it's not the same for me?" Arrow mentioned the last concern first.

"Do you want him to have all the things in life he wants?"

"Yes, how do I do that?"

"I think you know and there's very little reason in denying him what he wishes unless you have feelings for someone else," he eyed her suspiciously.

"No," it had always been Tib, the only person she truly knew she loved.

"Then what's the problem?"

"He expects things of me," she lowered her eyes to the food she had yet to touch.

"How do you know that those things are an experience you don't want?"

Her eyes questioned though her thoughts continued. "I wasn't trying to start a family of…us."

"Ah," he wiped his mouth with a hand, "I have no way of knowing what's going to happen genetically, maybe we're incompatible for breeding and need scientific intervention, but I doubt it." He folded his large hands in front of him on the table.

"I don't want to know."

"Tell Tib that then," he stood and left, only leaving her with more questions. Why did this have to be so hard?

"Arrow?" Flint stood at her side with his own food, "are you alright?" he sat across from her with Blade next to him.

She had been staring at her apple for a while, "Yes I'm alright, hello Blade." She smiled at her.

"We just built a dozen foundations, not completely but nearly and she is so smart," he pointed a thumb at Blade who pretended not to hear him and started eating.

"That's great," Arrow stood up to leave, "See you later guys."

After she had walked away Flint was unsettled, "She didn't eat anything," Blade shrugged it off. He wasn't going to let it go that easily, "Do you think it was us?" she seemed to ignore him but he knew something was wrong.

~~

Bow would be on the farms for the next two nights and she was staying in the bunks with the girls for the time being so she wouldn't be lonely. When he got back though he'd expect an answer and it wouldn't do for her to pretend to want what she didn't really. How could she let him down gently?

The next day Arrow stood in the kitchen of the mess hall shucking corn as Blade came in.

"I had to find out why you left the table when we sat down last night," Blade looked offended.

"Do you really care?"

"I think I do." She sat down on the stool Arrow never used, "Flint's told me several stories where you saved his life or lit a fire in the rain. You mean a great deal to him."

"That boy tells too many stories. You'd think he's some kind of historian." She shredded the husk from the corn in her hand and kept moving through the rest of the bushel. In the months since they'd arrived she had settled into a split schedule of cultivation and preparation. Keeping busy was her only escape from the eyes she felt watching her, wondering what she knew, even though she didn't actually know anything else at all.

"He spoke to Steel about interviewing you for a book. He wants to write about how you saved us all."

"I did no such thing." She looked all around them in the kitchen but they were the only two there.

"No sense denying it to me," she pointed to the ornate C for Core tattooed on the front of her shoulder in the cut-off t-shirt she wore, something she designed after Bow jumped ship in the middle of the night. "I had five of my own pages Arrow."

"Without you he would have needed six strong minded men that I couldn't find." Blade was flattered but showed nothing, a trademark of all the Core group members, "Does Flint already know?"

She shook her head matter-of-factly, "We took an oath, each of us, to reveal sources to no one and credit intuition for our foresight and luck."

"Steel wanted faith, he's got it." Arrow was impressed.

"Why, then, did you walk away?"

"Can I trust your confidence?"

"I don't think I need to go over this again." Arrow nodded but still hesitated.

"Bow wants to have a formal bonding ceremony but I… well I'd rather we just remain as we are without the spectacle he proposed."

"Are fifteen years somehow insufficient for a bond?" Blade truly looked perplexed by the conversation.

"He wants to have it in the square and invite everyone in the entire place."

Blade took her hand, "You love him and he is so happy about it he'd invite the whole world and for all I know he has."

"Will Flint hate me though?"

"You're the center of his world too but he just wants you to be happy."

"Goodness, am I going to be a wife? Bow's little woman?"

"Yes, his insanely intuitive, stronger than iron, wife who this entire Port should worship the way Bow wants to."

"That is insane, I simply had a plan."

"You had to run to the coast to get Strobe and Timber to help us. Before you even knew why, you created the only family I've ever had and you made a leader of a lost man."

"I did?"

"Flint wants to know about those travels and maybe he should but you are always going to love Bow." With that, Blade left to get to her job, satisfied that she had an answer for Flint

~~

He was due back any time now so Arrow sat outside the gate on a huge boulder and waited. When he showed up he was with Timber and she held her tongue.

"There she is," Timber grinned, "Have you accepted yet?"

"Don't tell him first," Bow shoved, "I'll be jealous." He kissed her cheek taking her down from the rock with an arm around her waist and set her to the ground. Timber just laughed and went in through the gate.

"Would you like an answer?"

"Only if it's a yes," he kissed her neck before letting her out of his strong arm.

"Yes, I will go through with a ceremony, we'll have to figure something out so no one will notice me but I will."

"Now I have everything I've ever wanted, we're safe with one another forever."

"Can you ever physically bond to me, like someone from here?"

"I've been in love with you half of my life, forget being different for once and see that you are perfect." He swept her up in his arms and kissed her gently, "I'm going to tell Steel to start spreading the news." He carried her inside to where Flint stood waiting.

"Blade said you wanted to bond."

"We will, she's accepted." Tib was elated, booming out his pride.

"Congratulations," he smiled and Arrow knew how right Blade had been.

"I think you should represent both of our families." Bow had a point, "Someone should stand with you as well, would Blade support us?"

Flint nodded, "We'll build your house personally, make a new custom for Port."

"A place outside," Bow set her down again, "I can't believe you want to build us a home."

"Arrow, if anyone deserved a place outside it's you," he hugged her for the third time since they'd known one another. "Now what are the colors to be?"

She shrugged and Bow laughed, "She's not going to make this easy on me will she?"…

## Chapter 9

"Find Arrow!" Flint screamed over the gathering crowd as he carried Bow's motionless body in through the west gate. Steel bolted to find her in the mess hall where she was chopping fruit for later that evening.

"Bow's hurt," The words sounded foreign, she shook her head and kept chopping, "Come on Arrow, he's hurt badly." He took nearly all of her forearm in one of his huge hands, "It didn't look good." Finally she looked at his eyes and realized how serious he was.

She pulled his hand from her and started to run before realizing she had no idea where to go, "Show me," the panic in her voice reached her eyes and he led her at a run to the mass of concerned citizens, now completely surrounding the scene. She heard someone whisper that he was dead and closed her eyes as Steel urged her through the horde.

In the center she saw him, bloodied and broken but breathing shallowly still, she dropped to her knees taking his head in her lap. His gray eyes focused on her face, he whispered out a harsh and singular word, "forever" and she felt him sigh out his last breath. She shook him once, hoping to rouse him but he didn't move again. The heart wrenching cry that exploded from her was proof enough to the crowd that he was dead. She straightened his tattered and bloody clothes and kissed his lips one last time, hardening with each passing second. The tears weren't coming, the sorrow was only building her from the inside, mortar and stone layer upon layer.

Steel began to suggest people move along to their jobs or beds, Flint hadn't moved or spoken a word since she arrived, hunched and shaking he stared at her as she closed up and tried his best to remember the places she was burying herself. "What happened to him?" Steel asked Flint quietly so she wouldn't hear them.

"He fell from the top of the quarry and caused a slide, I don't know what he was doing up there," he looked confused and grieved and helpless. Steel lifted him back to his feet by an elbow.

"Help me carry him to the infirmary," Flint nodded and they walked over to Arrow. Steel patted her shoulder and lifted his body from her. She didn't move staring at the ground, soaked in his blood. In less than a minute from seeing him surrounded by the entire residence of the Port, she was alone with his blood. The world meant nothing, color drained from it as she brooded, the red on her hands faded to black.

"Arrow?" Flint's voice jolted her out of her own turmoil. "Come with me, let me help you."

"Can I still stand and walk, am I not dead with him?" her eyes brimmed with tears as he helped her to her feet.

"We're alive, why would he have been on top of the quarry?"

"How should I know?" she shoved him away from her.

"I'm sorry, I only thought you would be the one...," she pulled her knife from her belt strap and turned on him, "Whoa."

"Why don't you know?" she held the gleaming blade to his throat, "You dragged him home Flint, why don't you know?" the tip of her knife broke his skin, she pulled away about to apologize when it stopped bleeding and closed.

"I can explain," Her jaw dropped, "I really can, stay calm."

"Who are you?"

"That's new. Most people say 'what' am I."

"I'm delusional, this isn't happening," she walked, dazed away from him to the infirmary dropping her knife somewhere along the way, Flint watched, wanting to follow her and wanting to help if he could.

"Arrow," Steel hugged her tightly, "I'm so sorry,"

"I need to stay with him for a moment." He nodded letting her go. Behind a swinging door Tibur was laid out on a table, uncovered. She saw so many slices through his skin, one large puncture wound obvious on his chest that must have been the killing point. He looked so fragile, no...she corrected herself, he was broken and gone. She took up an empty bucket and filled it with clean water, pulling off his shirt and cleaning his wounds. She would be alone forever but it was worse still because no one could ever understand how much she wished to join him in death. Crawl into his coffin and be buried next to her parents with him and Rage. Everyone she loved, no... Anyone who loved her was bound to die. After she'd washed all of him and redressed him in the plain clothes from the dresser in the room, she set his hands over his chest and held them in her own.

"It's been an hour, you should get some air," she nodded, patting Bow's hands gently as she left.

"I loved him Steel, what God hates me so much as to take him from me, who's angry with me?"

"You've done nothing to deserve this, you're a good person."

"I can't even properly kill myself."

He took hold of her shoulders, wanting to shake her, wanting to scream at her for being so selfish, "You can't wish such a thing, not in front of me. I'm your...friend and I won't allow such thoughts."

"WHAT HAVE I?"

"People who care about you are everywhere."

"Send me away and protect them from themselves."

His face went soft, "What will I do without my best friend?"

"I'm already gone," she thought of Flint healing in front of her eyes, that couldn't have been real unless...

"You can't be gone, Flint needs you and so do I."

She nodded, "Can I make arrangements in the morning, I can't think anymore today?" she sat down on the ground next to his feet.

"Of course you can, unless you don't want to deal with it anymore at all."

"I was supposed to be bonded to him in three weeks. Now he'll be in the ground without me forever."

~~

A month later Arrow took her first night off. Bow was in the ground and she did her best to block all feeling by staying on night shifts. Outside of the walls for the first time in thirty days was far less than thrilling but she had to visit his grave.

"Mind if I tag along?" Flint caught up to her, she hadn't seen him either but she suspected Steel kept him informed if he asked about her.

"No," she shook her head and kept walking. He was more accustomed to this side of her than any other and found himself comfortable. It was five miles before she spoke, "How's Blade?"

"She's been with Timber a lot since I stopped building your house. He's leading a few bigger projects and she was interested."

"You stopped building everything didn't you?"

"I needed to talk to you about what you saw," he swallowed audibly and she stayed silent, "I don't know why I heal and I'm sorry I didn't tell you. Steel knew right away but he promised not to say anything to you or anyone else." He was rambling and she wanted him to stop.

"I don't care about that, you have nothing to explain." That was enough for her she didn't want an apology nor would she accept one. He didn't need to know about her yet. He never should, if she could help it or else he would connect even closer with her. She didn't want anyone else in her life, not even the ones who already were.

"I thought you hated me," He confessed as they reached the graveyard. Most of the markers were in memory of whole families lost to the orphans of Port. Bow was up on the ridge just above the very quarry where they shared all of their secrets.

"You didn't do anything, he fell. I'm sure you would have helped if there was any way to save him." At the top of the hill she sat next to his burial mound. "Hello Tib, sorry it took me so long." She set a few loose rocks on top.

"May I sit with you?"

"Can't expect you to walk ten miles and not sit down," she gave a faint smile then looked back to the world below them, "He liked you anyway."

"I wish I could have done something to help him, I'd give this to him if I could."

"No, he was perfect how he was. He did so much in his life he deserved a better death, but accidents happen to everyone."

"Steel told me you lost your bunk mate before any of this happened, how?"

"Rage was a bit spontaneous. She tried once to jump off of the roof but Steel saved her then one day she built this huge bonfire out back of the group home and managed to blow herself sky high with crackle bark."

"Exploding trees grow around here?"

"They did for a while, Steel had them moved to the North before we broke ground," she pointed, "Rage is next to the lake there," he saw a large concrete block that he couldn't identify from the distance and nodded.

"Where are your parents?" again she pointed to a big block placed in the distance, "Why so far apart?"

"Wouldn't want them to be unhappy, Rage went fishing every day of her childhood so the lake made sense. My parents wanted to be together in the valley so there they lie and Tibur always loved this quarry as much as I did. Someday I want to be right here." She laid herself back into the sparse grass and dirt next to Tib.

"And for your life?" she looked at him a little dazed like she didn't understand.

"What?"

"Your life Arrow, there is a great deal of it left to live?"

"I don't know anymore. I was ready to live it for once now I resent the possibilities for the impossibility of him."

"I've cared about you for a long time."

"That's very sweet Flint but you're too young."

"I'm thirty. I think the healing and aging have something to do with one another." Now she was angry and he saw it. "How could I tell you when I look so young?"

"I should have you publicly shamed for your lies, but it can't be done without exposing you for what you are."

"Steel thought you could handle this but I don't agree anymore."

"You've been lying to me since we met. I bet you remember your name as well."

"I do, but it's meaningless to me."

"Tell me!"

"Bolt, I had a family. Mother, father and a couple of brothers that all died in detonation but I woke up dirty and perfectly fine or terrified and mostly fine I mean, my foot was spun around on my ankle. I fixed it and started searching burned out houses for survivors and no one, just pieces and nothing." She laid there for a long time in the dirt next to his mound without saying another word, digesting the massive mess Flint had made for himself.

"I prefer Flint."

"Me too," He looked at her, "can you ever forgive me?"

"Already have, had I lost everyone that day I would have changed my name as well."

"About us?"

"We are friends but I won't return your sentiment, never told Bow, I can't tell you either."

"You did love him though?"

"With every thought in my mind and cell in my body, he completed me and I like to think I did the same for him." They sat together another long time in silence.

"There is something else."

"What's that?"

"I found a letter that Tib must have written while you were away and it mentioned your ability. What's that?"

"I don't know," she lied.

"Alright, I'll speculate if I have to." She looked amused and sat up. "You are psychic?"

"No,"

"Telepathic?"

"No,"

"I could do this the entire walk back you know."

"I don't want you to know what it is."

"Do you heal like me?" he saw her face change almost suspiciously, "Its true isn't it?"

"What difference does it make?"

"What difference, I thought I was alone in the world and too different for anyone to care about and you heal too?"

"I still don't want to start anything like what I just lost."

"Arrow," he looked wounded, "I wasn't suggesting we bond, you loved Bow. He was your partner, something I never imagine being worthy of but I'll always be here for you."

She raised a hand to stop his talking, "You'll end up right here too if you have real feelings for me. Live your life without me."

"Then you are leaving, I thought Steel was being dramatic."

"You don't know him at all if you think he'd joke about someone leaving." She bent down pulling some wildflowers and placing them on his grave.

"Where will you go?"

"The other two coasts of course, send people here to our new society and wander forever."

"I'll go with you, keep you safe and help convince anyone we find."

"You've done enough for me, make a life here."

"Reject me, me?" He was less angry than hurt.

"What are you suggesting anyway? Steel is resisting my leaving in the first place, there's no way he'll let me take you."

"He's not going to stop either of us, we aren't bound to him." Her hand came up so fast he couldn't dodge the sharp slap to his cheek.

"I'm bound to no one," she growled through gritted teeth.

"I'm sorry, I didn't mean it that way."

"Stay behind me or I'll hit you again."

"Damn it, you can't be mad at me now, I meant we don't have to stay anymore."

"I don't, you could leave too if you wanted but not with me." One last look at Bow's pile of rocks, 'Goodbye my love' a fresh hole in her heart, "I'll be alone as I should have been all along."

"Alone?" he remembered the letter he read even better than before, "When you left before you were mad at Tib? What happened?"

"He was convinced I'd never come back and didn't want me to go alone."

"And you went anyway?"

"Yes,"

"That seems like a terrible way to leave things."

"It's none of your business. I had to leave to save them all. He was not an exception and he was safe here. I knew where I was going wasn't safe at all."

"I still want to know where you went one day, how you survived so long on the move."

"You saw firsthand, I know plants and trees and I'm strong."

"And you heal like me, didn't you wonder about me?" He followed at a distance like she asked him to and couldn't see her face, "I was terrified you would figure me out." She stopped abruptly and turned to him.

"You're always going to be afraid someone will see, only Steel is smart enough to stay covered."

"Steel too huh?" she nodded, "I should have known."

"So you're leaving too?"

"With you," he said forcefully, "I go with you from now on."

"Fine," she huffed, he caught up and they finished their walk without speaking again.

## Chapter 10

"Look Steel, I can't stay around here. It's enough to know you all stuck together." She turned around to look him in the eye, something snapped as their gazes met.

"There's no more Bow so nothing to tie you down huh?" He reached out to grab her hand, "What about me? Did you think I wasn't affected by you leaving us here to figure this out?"

"Let me go." she said gently tugging but he wasn't letting go.

"Arrow, I want you."

"Be serious Steel."

He took her arm, spun her around to pin her back against his chest, "I'm very serious and I know how strong you are."

"Steel please." His fingers went lax but she hesitated to pull away. He bent down over her shoulder where she turned meeting his lips. She couldn't compare it to Bow, the feeling with him had always been safety. Steel was hot and heavy, his fingers crept into her hair. His tongue slipped in between her lips, drinking from her confusingly eager and timid mouth. She sighed as he dropped both hands.

"You kissed back?"

"You kissed me." She was still a little stunned but managed to shove away.

"I didn't, for twenty years, everyone has their limits."

"This is very literally the strangest thing I've ever experienced and I've seen most of my bones jutting out of my body." The door at the far end of the room came open and they moved further apart before they could see who was coming in.

"Steel, there are a couple of produce exchanges going on out here and Willow doesn't like the requests. Hello Arrow."

"Hi Timber," She patted Steel's arm and started towards the door.

"I'll catch up with you later." Steel sat at his desk and turned his attention to the sheet of numbers that was handed to him.

"What was that all about?" Timber asked because he'd never seen that shade of red on Arrow's face before.

"I see Willow's issue right here," He circled a group of figures, ignoring the question and fixing the math, "Take her that and see if Flint is somewhere nearby, I need to talk to him."

"Sure," Timber waited a moment, hoping for further explanation. "I'll get on it then."

The room was empty again and Steel couldn't resist thinking about the kiss. She definitely kissed back and if he was to guess, she'd enjoyed it.

She didn't punch him or look angry when he'd pulled back to let her go. He needed to assure she wouldn't leave, maybe that wasn't the way he intended to broach the conversation but it was a solid opening argument. Someone knocked. "Come on in."

Flint peeked around the door, unsure what the room was. "Hey Steel, you wanted to see me?"

"Arrow wants to leave Port."

"Oh?" he looked confused but shut the door behind him anyway.

"She thinks that because Bow is dead she doesn't belong here."

"Are you asking me something or telling me it's time to leave?"

Steel stood, "You should talk to her, maybe see if you can change her mind because we need her. I've kept this situation under wraps for quite a while so I expect you to do the same."

"Of course, what's happening?"

"We've found another colony, not as well prepared with food but far better armed. We've got plenty of food but I'd like it to be a trade."

"You want to begin trading with a starving colony?"

Steel nodded and turned towards the window. "I was willing to ask for small weapons, hand lasers and rifles, but they refused saying we would only attack them when they were hungry again."

"Sound reasoning," Flint shrugged placing himself into one of the arm chairs across the wide oak desk.

"I started to offer them seeds as a way to begin their own growing but we're pretty far along and they wouldn't even have seedlings by the time winter began."

"Why not take them in?"

"That's the step I want to take but I want most of us out of here before I let the others in."

"So what does any of this have to do with her?"

"They'll take her in or hurt her if she travels into their land so I want you to get her to stay."

"How?" Flint looked even more confused.

"Tell her the situation or help her find love, make up a project. I really don't care how you do it."

"You want me to lie to her?"

"I gave you the option of telling her the truth." Steel shrugged.

"Okay, well love isn't going to happen but she's great at projects and enjoys helping people."

Arrow opened the door, "Hey guys," she smiled at Flint and let it fade as she turned to Steel. "Willow was closing up this big crate and wouldn't tell me where it was headed. Do we have a problem?"

Steel swore under his breath, "Just a little sharing with another colony."

She froze in the doorway, "Colony? Is it nearby?"

"Arrow, please don't even think about going out to meet them."

"Well, I'm going to go see how Strobe is doing with those new boxes." Flint practically ran from the room.

"They're armed to the teeth Arrow and I don't think any of them have seen a woman since detonation. They grabbed Pine and Timber nearly had to break the guys arm to get her back...You wanted me to lead this Port, keep us safe and try to figure out what we should do to move on."

"So we're all moving on?"

"I've been clearing out the caves. We have to move them there and let the hostiles take over Port for a while."

"They don't know how many people are here do they?"

"Not at all, I bluff on every direct question of capacity as well." He sat in the chair Flint had vacated.

"The whole thing sounds a little confusing."

"Arrow?" he reached for her hand but she pulled it away. "They've threatened to strip the trees bare and steal everything."

"We'll fix this somehow. Maybe it's time we send someone to the exploding trees." He was on his feet in an instant, "Not me." she defended. His hands on her cheeks felt so tense, gently his thumb rubbed along her lower lip.

"When we lost Rage I knew you were with her and I noticed you didn't come back with your favorite belt."

"It burned while I stripped the rest of my clothes."

"Why didn't you die?" he let his hand slide down to her neck, his thumb tipping her chin up to meet his eyes.

"I tried." He knew just what she meant. They'd both collapsed inside without ever letting it show. His kiss was soft her eyes closing slowly as he strung it out in smooth rhythms that hummed under her skin.

"She wasn't like us, neither was Tibur and now it's time to be together."

"What about Flint?"

"He knows you don't love him, maybe that's enough for us to be together nearly with his blessing."

"No," she backed away again, "No, we're too alike."

"Arrow?" she could hear the desperation in his voice. "Don't resist this any more than you have to. I won't let you disappear into the woods without me again." His tone had changed to warning and she got an uncomfortable knot in her stomach.

"Are you threatening me?"

"Maybe I'm just letting you know what's going to happen."
Her pulse quickened and he could feel her begin to heat up.

"No one owns me." she said through gritted teeth.

"You have me wrapped around your finger like a little
puppy and I won't lose you because you're the one for me."

"I loved Bow, you know that."

"He loved you too but now he's gone and I don't know if
you realize, but you're still here."

"I know I'm alive but there isn't anything left Steel. I don't
care about anything anymore. No one matters and I don't
want to help you lead who's left."

"So we don't stay, let them govern themselves and make
decisions."

She looked disappointed in him, "I guess I chose wrong
then."

"I was the right builder and mayor to start everything up
around here but the platform has changed and they need to
find a way to handle it because I don't know what to do."

"Can we sabotage the boxes to scatter them out on the prairie?" Surprised by the idea, he nodded an agreement before leaving the room in a rush.

~~

She finished nailing the last crate shut and turned around to Flint's smile.

"This is a really good idea."

"I don't know if it'll work but at least we can try." she dusted her hands of the saw dust that stuck to the sweat.

"Who are you sending...I mean who has Steel picked for the aftermath?"

"No one, we're going in ourselves."

"Absolutely not, you can't go out there and into their compound, that's crazy." He sounded panicked.

She couldn't stand it anymore, "There is nothing you're capable of doing or saying that could stop me." She set her jaw.

"Don't test me, please." Everything she had assumed about Flint faded slightly when she saw the fire light behind his eyes. "Pine says they have bombs and grenades I have never even heard of before, there is no way I'm letting you go without me."

"Who said we were?" She winked, tossing him the hammer.

"Good, I thought I might have to put my foot down."

"Whatever you have to tell yourself," she said walking away.

"If I insisted, would you really tell me no?"

"Absolutely, then Steel would set you onto a never ending task for penance of arguing with my authority." He started to challenge her when Crate and Timber walked up. "These are ready to go onto the cart if you can lift them." She watched the two of them easily take the freight away.

"Are you staying here Arrow, to help him or do you have another reason?"

"One has to be handled before the other can happen."

"I'm going with you then too."

"Good luck with that." She bent to lift the side of a crate, "Help me with this would you?" Flint tripped over himself to get there and they carried it to the wagon.

<u>Chapter 11</u>

That night Steel opened the east gate and the three of them slipped out behind the wagon leaving Pine in charge until their return.

"Fill me in on the plan here Steel." Flint walked with him leading the horse and watching for holes in the road.

"Arrow's going to try to get focus onto her and we'll sneak around to the other entrance and wait until they go to sleep, then she'll let us in and we disable as many weapons as we can."

"How do you do that?"

"You've never jammed up a gun before?"

"I'd never even seen one until I met Arrow." he glanced back at her watching the road for anyone sneaking up on them.

"Here," Steel handed him the spare weapon in his coat pocket. "The easiest way is to break the lens over the beam but there are many other ways too so take good care of that one."

"Yeah," he answered in a stunned, slow voice.

"We aren't hurting anyone Flint, but you can't go in unarmed." Arrow caught up to comfort him.

"Where's your gun?" He scanned her and noticed nothing stood out from her figure.

"I can't get in with a weapon, you have to keep me safe and listen to the rumblings to get to me as soon as you can."

"Hell no, let me distract them instead."

"Yeah I'm sure you're a perfect substitute for a woman but Arrow already made contact."

"Sending her into the lion's den?"

"Give me a break Flint. This is all we've got to work with to strip their weapons away." Steel was getting angry with the conversation, he was just as protective of her as Flint and it wasn't fair that he compared their relationships.

"No, she could get hurt in there."

"No I can't."

Flint's head whipped back to Steel, "That's just what we think, we don't know." Arrow walked with the wagon leaving them to talk about her. "What if they torture her Steel?"

"I've made it through that and she can too." Flint ran after Arrow to catch up.

"I don't care if you are invincible. I still don't want you to go in there unarmed." He pulled a butterfly knife from the shreds of leather he called a boot. She spun it over her fingers and stuck the thin metal into her hip belt.

"Thanks." she kissed his cheek and moved on.

"Are you Steel's girl now?"

"No," She remembered Steel pulling her in for a firm and warning kiss. "He thinks he can change our relationship into something else but I think he's wrong"

"You're thinking about it."

"Damn it Flint,"

"What?"

"He doesn't have any idea what a connection is or what I had with Bow or what I have with you."

"You're my only friend here Arrow, if that's how you say it is then I believe you."

"He's not what I want, let's get this place contained and leave them all behind us Flint."

"Are you joking?"

"Yes." Steel finally caught up and the two of them stopped talking completely.

Steel spoke first after a minute's long silence, "Are we all still on plan?"

"We're ready but I still don't like her going in."

"Flint, neither do I but she's sure to be fine."

"Enough," she quietly stopped them. "I'm not going in alone, both of you are going to be right outside." Steel suggested they take a break and sat with Arrow and the horse.

"You know, I would be really upset if anything happened to you so please stay safe in there."

"I'll be fine, don't worry about me."

"Don't exactly think that's an option anymore, years of concern for your safety and want of your company have made you a permanent fixture in my mind."

"I guess that's nice." She stroked the horse's mane as she stood up.

"Would you ever think of being my bride?" She didn't say a word, she didn't wait a second. Arrow stepped out from behind the head of the beautiful paint horse and hit Steel with her full force in the mouth. He licked blood from his lip and nodded his head, "Yep, I deserved that."

Flint popped up from his sleeping spot behind the wagon seeing Steel rubbing at a rapidly growing bruise on his cheek and remembered when she had slapped him. "Everything okay you two?"

"Yes, thank you Flint." Arrow answered a bit frustrated with her situation. "Now I'm going to sleep, don't bother being the one who wakes me," she walked towards Flint and pulled out her roll to lie down. Flint took second watch and stayed next to Arrow on the ground to keep Steel from getting himself hit a second time. She was no longer taking any of their advances and Flint was proud of her for it, a girl like Arrow didn't need to be with anyone unless she actually wanted to be.

The three of them came up upon the settlement of hostiles at the first light of dawn. Anticipation and fear grew in Steel the closer they got. Though his bruise was already healed every glance at Arrow reminded him of the savage blow she'd dealt him. With the way she hid her feelings he hadn't noticed how much she was still struggling with her grief.

The leader of the colony stood at a makeshift wooden fence with a rifle over his dirty shoulder and a squinted eye. "Brought all the stuff you promised us then." He spit into the dirt at Steel's feet.

"We have some of the requests you made but we aren't a grocer." He passed the angry man a packing slip Willow had hand printed.

"What about the women?"

"My people aren't up for trade or any kind of sale." Flint set his feet, anticipating a fight from them.

"I know, but I'd hoped maybe some would want to come along." He rolled up the page and put his hand out to Steel, "Name's Trigger."

"Steel, this is Flint and Arrow."

"Ah, Arrow has arrived. I have two of my own who met you a long time ago."

"What are their names?"

"Shadow and Freight," Arrow smiled remembering them both fondly with a nod. "They'll be glad you're here for a few days."

"Are we coming inside to unload or do we just drop it here?"

"I'll get the guys." he kicked the wooden fence with his heel. "We have some strong guys around here."

"I'm sure." Steel stepped back behind the cart and tucked his weapon into his coat, prompting Flint to do the same. Three large men exited a separation in the fence, lifted the huge crates and disappeared inside again.

"Are you staying to eat Steel?"

"No, we'd best be heading back." Arrow turned to hug Flint, sent Steel a salute and vanished with Trigger behind the fence. "This doesn't feel right."

"Keep walking Steel, they're watching us to make sure we leave. They won't hear us come back later."

"She was tense."

"Of course, she's only safe though if we play this right."

"Why are you more sure than I feel?"

"She told me to be the strong one..."

She watched them doze off, pretending to be tired as well, the sleeping drought in the milk was genius and adding it to the water was only an afterthought but a good call since most of them needed that far more than the food.

Those that weren't sleeping were starting to find places to bed down. She slid herself down a plank to sit in a tuft of grass. After a long time she glanced around and everyone she saw was fast asleep. Arrow tapped the coded message she taught them onto the wooden fence and stood to catch the weapon Steel tossed over to her. Carefully, Arrow crept around the colony that was little more than a camp, pulling firing sights and smashing lenses as she worked her way to the gate.

Flint was over the wooden barricade with a light landing and Steel followed close behind. A look set them in separate directions and it wasn't long before Steel found the stockpile and whistled them over.

"There aren't a whole lot of these grenades we should take some for ourselves."

"We can't steal from them Flint." Arrow hissed as she unscrewed the cap of the metal ball, exposing the gray powder. "Open them up and mix it with this." She showed him a little bag of powder and started to explain it to them when they heard a rustling in a bush nearby.

"I'll check it out," Steel crouched down and vanished into the half light of the dying day.

"Come on Flint we may be losing time." She destroyed the mixtures of the grenades and set them back into the milk crates like they were before. Flint finished the last gun and turned his focus to scanning for Steel, when they heard another whistle.

A shadowed figure waved them to a dark wall, Steel had someone with him, "Slower, I don't feel right about this." Flint took her arm to keep pace with her steps and look natural as they checked the situation closer. "Is that one of the two you know?"

"I can't tell," she whispered back as they slunk towards them.

"Wait, its Strobe." They jogged the rest of the way and Strobe tried not to look at them funny, turning his head to smirk about it.

"We're setting up to leave," He nodded with a smile as they got to him.

"Is everyone ready to move?" Flint asked.

"We're all packed and the canning year set us up pretty well for food."

"Move to the caves Strobe." Steel gave the order and returned the nod he received. Strobe bound the fence in a step, it seemed.

"Are we clear Arrow?"

"Get the guards weapon and then we're gone." Flint was already there, pulling at the dangling gun. Arrow saw Trigger lumbering over with anger and menace in his eyes and called out to him, "Blaze a trail Flint."

He spun around, catching Trigger in the head with his elbow and taking him down. "Thanks." he hopped the fence into the dark.

"Is he always so cocky?" Steel asked with a chuckle she smiled her own answer and made her way over the fence herself followed a moment after by Steel.

"Head to the mountains through the reeds and don't leave a trail or at least no tracks. I'll be there tomorrow." He watched them off into the distance and saw Arrow reach to take Flint's hand as they faded away. After thinking about it for a moment he was glad Arrow was moving on, at least he hoped she was, he picked up his bag over his shoulder and walked in the pitch black, back to Port Harbor. He'd store more into the old orphanage and only leave scraps for those vultures to find. Pine and Willow had pickled and canned nearly round the clock for almost a month. When they realized they couldn't pack it all Steel had them bury a portion of it in the woods.

Steel kicked down East gate with a forceful blow, pissed about being moved out of his home, his first real home. He'd watched them do their parts as they built their place. He loved the damn walls and the dirt and all of the buildings and the way it buried his need to know where Arrow was. Love was complicated but if he stayed open...he'd end up right where he was now, smashing the walls of his own town so others couldn't use its safety. He wanted to burn it down but the idea turned his stomach.

## Chapter 12

"Cut north," Arrow hiked ahead of him on the long abandoned trail away from the mountains.

"Why aren't we meeting them?"

"Shut-up and follow me, if we drift off course we hit crackle forest.

"He isn't so bad you know, and we were helping him shut down that hostile bunch."

Arrow spun around, anger in her eyes enough that Flint took a half step back. "I swear to you that if you start kissing me and telling me I'm the one. I'll leave you behind too."

"Oh." It never occurred to him that she could be running from Steel. He must have used love as a way to make her stay, like he'd tried to tell Flint to do but he hadn't or maybe Steel's feelings were real. There was no way for him to know for sure.

"Cut north Flint." She sped up significantly and the best he could do was keep up. It was hours before she stopped.

"Water?" he groaned at the waves he heard before he saw them.

"We're in a coastal area. We'll follow the shore for a while now."

"Can I take a break?" She nodded, breaking a branch from a Cyprus tree to sharpen with her knife. "Would Steel hunt people down?"

"Bow stole a lot of food and he wasn't all that far away from Port so I don't think so."

"You aren't Bow," he looked at her a little closer than he normally would, trying to find that smiling face from the picture he'd brought back for her. Looking for the hopeful woman that he'd walked to Port with all those days and hours.

"We are free people, un-sworn and we're free to live wherever we choose."

"All I know is he has a lot on his plate right now, then tomorrow he'll have two more scoops on that plate."

"I don't care. He can't keep pushing me to feel something I don't and I don't want to discuss this again."

"Arrow was the reason Port existed, who are you?" Flint tossed a leaf to the ground.

"I'm Stone."

"Flint and Stone, we could easily start a fire." he tried to joke.

"We are a fire. We burn everything we touch except one another." She grinned, "I'm hungry." She left him to fish in the waves.

Flint hated the empty pit he had for a stomach but he respected her too much to let her be alone in the world. Arrow would take care of him and he would watch after her.

"Start a fire."

"How?" He glanced around at the wet sand and rising tide with a fair amount of doubt that she would find anything either.

"Climb the palm tree, pull down the dry stuff. Come on Flint it hasn't been that long since we were on the road."

"I never expected to do this again." He was already half the way up the trunk of the palm tree he'd been leaning against.

"Me either, but at least we're together and it's familiar even though it's not."

"I'm more afraid of hostile people." He cut huge fronds from the dry bottom branches of the tree.

"We can take care of them if they come along."

Fed and less pessimistic, Flint took her hand as they watched the waves roll in in the dark. "Should we find our own place or are we going full on nomad?"

"I want to find an apartment in the middle of a big city and stay there until we can't stand it anymore." Her grip tightened on his fingers.

"Anything you want, absolutely anything." Flint promised her.

"Do you still feel guilty for leaving?" He shook his head, "good, because being out here without you would be much harder."

"Can I still call you Arrow?"

"Yes, but not if we meet people, then we're Stone and Blaze."

"You're still my best friend and the only person I would do this for." She squeezed his hand and let it go.

"Goodnight," The old routine was right back in place, she curled up to his chest and slept for the first part of the night, then took second watch so he could sleep most of every night. She didn't sleep much when they were in the open. That's when he realized he may be the only person left in the world who really knew her anymore.

~~

"Did Arrow and Flint arrive alright?"

"They aren't with you?" Pine looked confused, "I just assumed you three would arrive together." She stepped to the side letting him into the entrance of their new mountainside home.

"Where are they?" he turned back to the entrance and Pine began a morbid guessing game.

"The hostiles could have captured them or they got caught in bear traps or they just left again. You know how famous Arrow is for taking off when she's needed."

"I don't know why you dislike her so much but that's not what she's doing at all. She just lost Bow and it's probably painful to be around any of us."

"So you're going to follow her?" he nodded, "Her name should have been target."

"Are you jealous?"

"Yeah, maybe I am, no one is ever wondering where I am or if I'll survive each little stumble in my life"

"Why don't you tell Crate you want to bond with him?"

"Because I'm too busy making sure everyone is safe and happy around your Port." Steel shook his head gravely.

"It's time to care about what's most important to you. These people can get by without our everyday guidance. Go and show Crate how you feel." She walked outside to her post thinking about what he said and wondering when he would leave.

The caves were an elaborate underground labyrinth of halls that ran under the old orphanage. No one knew what they were for or where they ended exactly but they were safe and hidden. His people were doing well adjusting to the new living arrangements but his heart was no longer in it.

"The hostiles are settling in as well as we are here, is there something wrong?"

"I need to leave Willow. Can you and Timber hold it together around here?"

"How long?"

"I don't think I'll come back." She nodded before ducking under the sheet he'd blocked his doorway with. A pack was already full of supplies and ready for him. No one would stop him but Pine wasn't letting it go so easily and stood at the exit he took out of the dark.

"Where are you going?"

"East for as long as I can and then north."

"She won't be there to find Steel, she's at least a thousand miles away." He set the pack down in the dirt. "I stopped you last time for us, now it's for you."

"I want to help her."

"Crate would chase me too but he'd already be gone."

"Does she ever plan on coming back or am I to be left behind like Bow?" Pine shrugged. "I'm an idiot."

"Yes, but for the right reason." she smiled before going to her post higher up the cliffs. Steel let the empty feeling go away and went back inside to his closed room.

<u>Chapter 13</u>

Six months, nine days and seventeen hours after she changed their plan and direction, he found their home. "Stone," it was the only name she answered to anymore.

"Yeah," her eyes searched the place as she came in.

"This is it." He dropped the pack he'd found in his second lost and found box, a favorite searching place of Flint's when they found a new building.

"It sure seems to be." The place was empty windows and open floors. It was ten flights of stairs from the lobby and they had come through a maze of halls to find it. All the locks on the doors were functional and there was a service elevator to an old laundry room in the basement. "We should find some furniture and set it up, candles and cubes for light..."

"Are you sure we're far enough away?" He nodded to reassure her and went to search more of the apartments and offices in the building.

Flint moved in a mattress he found on the seventh floor and a box spring from the fourth. She had started tossing the old residents photos down the laundry chute. "Should we stay in the same room?" he sat down on the counter next to where she stood.

"No, I want the room in the back." She tossed the last wrapped and topped box down the chute.

"Fair, can I get you something better than that pull out couch?"

"If we find it here, I keep seeing lights out there and we can't go out too far during the day either."

"So we hide here and starve to death?" She only looked at him without a real expression. "I know you can hunt and we have the small stock of cans but this can't last us."

"Make a suggestion Flint."

"Let's go home."

"Excuse me?"

"We should go to Port or the caves or anywhere near Steel and the rest of our friends where we're safe."

"That's a long trip to take all by yourself." He hopped down from the counter and left the room, "I'm not going back there Flint, ever."

"I'll go by myself then." A door slammed and she flinched. In all the time they'd spent together he never stormed off or argued with her but they had also never stopped together for a month, then another month, he hated the locked in feeling of the building.

On the roof he reached behind the vent pipe for the binoculars and scoped out the closest light in the city. It was a small fire but was burning all the time from an exposed natural gas line. The next light he focused on was set on a rooftop, he looked but didn't see anyone around it. The third was being held in a large hand as he scanned up the face it became all shadow and turned away. It felt familiar, the gait and breathing looked like Steel from this distance. Chances were good he hadn't followed them.

"I'm sorry I snapped at you."

"Forget that," he passed her the binoculars, "Due east." He pointed.

"Moving lantern in the green hooded hand is new." She examined him longer than Flint had. "Unfamiliar, he moves like Steel but he's taller."

"He's searching."

"But for who or what?"

"We can go find out if you want to." She shook her head sharply. "Arrow, he's pretty old."

"He carries three weapons."

"What?" She grinned, passing the lenses back.

"Hip slung hand-held gun, ankle strapped weapon and a sword on his back under the cloak.

"Damn, he's ready for war out there."

"We should be too but I hate the thought of hurting people."

~~

"They are fine Steel, they were before and they are now." Pine handed him the tin mug full of hot tea.

"I know, but she's angry with me this time and I'm pretty sure neither is coming back."

"So, she's capable of taking care of herself and you have enough to worry about."

"I'm going after her."

"No you aren't, we have less than a week before we'll have those hostiles on our doorstep." Her finger aimlessly pointed at the common room outside in the hall.

"They aren't anything to be scared of."

"Oh is that so? We're funneled into a hole in the mountainside and no one can fight any better than they can run away. They'll slaughter us and laugh at our corpses."

"Alright, I guess I can't abandon you when you need me." Pine nodded and left to go to sleep before her night watch. Steel began making plans behind her back. He asked Willow to stock him with more supplies and she helped him plot a course. It only made sense to plan it the way Arrow must have.

~~

"We're out of food and we still haven't found clean water. I think we should go to the people who left here."

"I'm not ready to give up, let's go up there though, maybe stir things up." Trigger cracked his neck and whistled over to a couple guys to come along. The hike was treacherous but Trigger didn't let up, pushing them the whole three hours. The makeshift shack Steel built on the cliff side was almost convincing enough to stay in but no one did for safety reasons. Pine stood in the door with a bit of a grimace on her not so kind face.

"What do you want?"

"So hospitable, poisoning people and breaking our weapons then just sweet enough to ask what we want," the sarcasm seeped from his lips like a poisonous fog.

"Do we look real cozy here or something to you Trigger?" Pine snapped at him.

"Not really but you ran from home, maybe it's time for a truce?" his smirk painted his face.

"I'll let you discuss that with Steel." she spun to the cave opening but Steel was already there. "These...gentlemen would like to talk with you."

"Thanks Pine," she stormed off through the maze like halls. "What brings you up the mountain? Getting a little sparse down there? We still aren't dangerous but we are creative. Have you found the water yet?"

"There isn't any."

"Not anything? Not even in the well if you pump it?"

"No, we aren't morons." Trigger's anger rose as Steel patronized him.

"You could have fooled me." He confidently tucked himself behind the desk he'd never sat behind before. "You threatened a huge scientific community looking for peace and they lashed back. You should really start thinking things through before you act."

"We aren't here to argue the past." Trigger growled.

"Steel, we're ready to move forward." A tall dark man spoke alongside Trigger.

Steel's hands went up. "What do you propose?"

"A truce that could lead to a blending of the families."

"Are you all willing to be sworn in and capable of respecting the laws?"

"Let's see the laws, so we aren't agreeing blindly." Trigger sat across from him at the old desk.

"It's simple. This is a community that we all work for and in. No one is against the collective."

"You're a bunch of hippies," He thought for a moment. "My men aren't ready to settle down just yet but how about we play security for you all from the west and you share food in return?"

"How can we trust you and what security do we need?"

Shadow stepped forward, "Had you given us the opportunity, our first trade would have been proof enough but you need security from the other three colonies."

"Three?" he was worried but not on the surface, "Can you still protect us without weapons?"

"We've got about a hundred rifles and at least fifty of our grenades that weren't tainted to explode." Steel preferred dealing with Shadow immediately, more civil than the crassness that seeped from Trigger.

"We could repair a few of the smaller weapons, if you agreed to keep us on your watch list."

"I think we could agree to that." He looked around, "Where's Arrow anyway?"

"She's out on another one of her goodwill missions, we expect her back any time now." he lied.

"We'll happily start our detail by escorting you back to your Port."

"I doubt that's necessary."

"Once we get out of there, we'll take some time to help out, at least help you get those gates back up." Steel agreed to some terms that worked for all of them before sending them back down the mountain. He told Pine what happened then sulked back to his room.

<u>Chapter 14</u>

(A week later)

Pine was finishing up some paperwork about all the trades and new citizens that would be entering Port when Crate peeked around the door, "Mind if I come in?"

"Not at all my love, how are you tonight?"

"You know, I'm pretty lonely. You're always so busy that we hardly even have dinner together anymore."

"You're pretty busy yourself but I know what you mean. What can we do?"

"Well, do you remember how Steel lifted the ban on bonding pairs?"

"Yes, I've looked at quite a few requests recently."

"You should add my request to the pile." Pine was stunned. He'd been so careful even after the ban was lifted to be nonchalant about how he felt for her. He hadn't even kissed her yet.

"Oh?"

"I want to be with you Pine, there's nothing else I really want anymore than to just be with you, to be your partner."

"Crate?"

"Please consider spending the rest of your life with me."

"I don't need to consider it, you're the only person I've ever wanted to be with and if you're asking me then yes." He swept her out of her chair and kissed her lips, so full of excitement for their future.

After a month of planning and moving themselves back into Port, Pine looked at herself in the only long mirror they had. She inspected her beautiful handmade dress and straightened her daisy crown around her black, shiny hair. Blade stood behind her for a moment in silence as she looked so deep in thought. "They're nearly ready for you out there."

Pine turned, taking slow steady breaths, "Thank you so much for this dress, it's perfect."

Blade smiled, "Couldn't think of a more wonderful bride to wear it, you two really are a great example of love for the ages."

"Oh, and thank you for helping me put this all together so quickly. With the new people and all the changes I was helping with I thought I would never get any of this ready in time."

"What are friends for?"

"That's so true, we've been friends since we were just little girls in that huge orphanage. You've been the only person I've shared most of my life with, I couldn't be happier that you're here today." Blade was beginning to feel uncomfortable. None of them had ever been very vocal about how they felt about anything besides the immense loyalty they showed one another. "Sorry, I'm getting all sentimental."

"No problem, it's your big day."

Timber poked his head into the room and smiled at the two dressed up ladies. "There's no time like now."

"Thanks Timber, I'm on my way." Pine looked at herself one more time, feeling happier than she had in all her life. "Here goes nothing."

Crate stood at the center of the square, surrounded by the residents of Port in rounded rows so everyone could see, dressed in a pressed black shirt and pants. He smiled the moment he saw Pine and her soft pink slip of a gown. She glowed with each step towards him. They were surrounded with love and support when she reached the small altar laid with a large bowl of clean water, two strips of silk cloth and a clean knife.

Silver stood from the crowd and took her place at the opposite side of the altar, lifting the knife and beginning the ceremony. "These two people have decided they cannot live without one another and wish to be bound forever. If any don't believe that they are worthy, speak now or bury your complaints with your body." She waited a few moments in silence then smiled lifting the knife. "Please put out your hands." They each reached towards her where Silver placed the shiny blade against the center of Crate's palm first, slicing towards his fingers then doing the same to Pine's. She set down the knife and guided their hands together, "repeat after me, 'Until the end of forever'."

"Until the end of forever." They both said with smiles on their faces as Silver rinsed out their wounds and handed them the cloths to wrap around their palms.

"These two souls are bound for eternity, neither shall come before their partner and none shall come between them." They raised their wounded hands together to cheers and congratulations from everyone. As the celebrations began and when she no longer thought she'd be missed, Blade snuck off to sulk near the mess hall.

"Blade," Steel noticed her in the dark a few minutes later.

"Yeah?"

"I was pretty sure I'd be the only sad face today." He sat down with her.

"I wanted to do this once, but now..."

"With whom?"

"Never mind."

"Blade, you can trust me."

"I don't know, maybe Flint would have asked me if Arrow found someone else."

"I love her Blade. Since I first saw her with her saw dust doll. We could help one another."

"How? They're gone?"

"We could find them, with your talent and my skills it would be easy, really."

"When do we leave?" she joked.

"How about I figure the details and you pack?" She nodded, beginning their partnership.

(Three weeks later and integrated at Port)

"Steel, Trigger has a few of the old buildings finished and ready for inspection."

"Thanks Shadow, can you send in Blade?"

"Sure thing," Shadow shut the door behind him and Steel shoved another knife into his full pack he kept concealed below his desk. When the door opened again he had his coat over the pack and a gun tucked into his ankle strap.

"Today's the day huh?" Blade locked the knob on the door.

"I have to find her, Pine said she plans to head to a big city. I bet she stopped in Philly."

"We're not coming back are we?"

"I doubt it, why?" Blade went over to the cabinet behind his desk and pulled out her full pack, slung it over her back and pulled a jacket on around it.

"Ready!" She zipped her jacket over the canvas bag.

"Let's go out at East gate to the coast all night." Steel led the way, casually talking about building material shortages and where they might find them. Blade took notes on a sheet of Willow's homemade paper as they made their way outside the towering walls of Port. They paused in the orchards while she filled a small bag with fallen fruit. No one noticed them leave the path and vanish into the trees...

Chapter 15

"Does he know how you feel?" He hadn't wanted to ask but it was hard not to.

"I told him that I held him in high respect."

"So, no." he laughed at her disappointed face. "Guys don't link respect to feelings in general. If you'd shown some leg or something." he shrugged.

"I didn't realize I wouldn't get to tell him before he left." she couldn't look up at Steel's face.

"Understandable, I missed out on Arrow for almost a dozen years but I never told her why I was always there for her."

"You were there for everyone."

"Because she wanted me to be," Blade stopped walking. "Do you see something?" he scanned the trees and ground around them.

"You saved us all for a girl?" she smiled at him as he nodded a little embarrassed. "I thought I knew all there was to know about our strong, walled up, fair Steel. That's amazing." She laughed.

"It's pointless if we never find her." She started walking again and they let the conversation drop as the ocean came into sight.

She slept while he took the first watch. The tide rolling onto the sand was relaxing his prickly nerves in the moonlight. He was surveying the trunks of the trees nearby when he saw the initials carved into the raised root.

F and B within a squared off heart, peeked above the waves at his right side. Flint may not have known her feelings but he had his own. The empty feeling Steel found himself fighting over and over, came back with a wave of nausea. Arrow hadn't deserved the forced pace he'd tried to set for them, she needed comfort and security to ease her into her confidence again and he'd grabbed at her like a wolf whistling moron. If he'd just thought for a moment he could have seen what was wrong then, now he was chasing a ghost for all he knew.

"Seen anything?" She yawned and stretched out.

"Yep," he pointed at the carving.

"Beautiful, and with the chisel I made him." She hid the smile but was truly happy to see it.

"He wasn't leaving you behind, took you every step of the way."

"I found where Arrow slept as well," Steel perked up a little. "Did she always scratch her mark?"

"Always," She showed him the windblown arrow in the dirt, "Wish I'd thought to bring a cube or two."

"Why?"

"To set it there and sleep where I can see it."

"What did you have when you were building?" Steel pulled his pack from his shoulders, reached into the front pocket and handed her the nearly worn through sheet of paper, she read it.

("You're the only person I can trust with this plan. I know we aren't close anymore and I'm sorry for that but you're the best person I know.")

Blade passed it back to him, "I held onto it because she never may have come back. When she did Bow was all she could think about. I guess it was my piece of her, the trust was all mine but her heart was his."

"Imagine being compared to her," she saw the sympathy cross his face before the worry. "What is it?" He signaled for her to stop talking and crouched down in the low brush.

"I see a wolf or a bear in the clearing over there, we need food." He pushed his back into the bushes and slid the laser gun from his hip. The beam was set to max when he hit the animal in the chest and watched it fall dead.

~~

The fires started four months after they settled into the building. He watched them burn closer every night.

"Are we still safe here, can we stay?"

"I think we've got another week before he gets here, he may skip this building like he did with the other two big ones." Flint looked at her, "They're hotels and no one lived in them. Maybe he's a clean freak who sleeps in a new bed every night."

His interest was piqued, "Oh?"

"Yeah."

"We've got to figure out what to do soon, I don't like feeling like a sitting duck."

"We...still?"

"In all the time it's been, I haven't made any other alliance, 'we' are all I've got."

"Good, tonight he'll go for the closed community and maybe find the old couple. Let's see what happens first."

"You think he'll kill them?"

"No, maybe he'll just take their food or leave them alone completely. Maybe he'll protect them," Arrow nodded at the nice suggestion, "Can't know until we see."

"Exactly, let's rest up to watch what happens." They sat there a long time on the roof of their building, wind whipping her hair around.

"Arrow, how do you really feel about Steel?" he'd never asked before, afraid she'd see it as interest or jealousy.

"That's a dual edged question because you know he pushed himself on me."

"There isn't anyone here besides us." Flint sat himself against the bricks of the emergency roof exit.

"I used to idolize him but once he kissed me, then he was just Steel, someone strong physically but incapable of the right restraint."

"If he apologized and gave you time?"

"Why do you want to know?" he shrugged but she wouldn't say another word until he answered her.

"If I bond with Blade I want to know you'll be happy as long as he gave you the time you needed."

"Maybe,"

"Can't the ideology come back on some level?"

"I guess only time will tell…why would me being with him make the difference?"

"Little promise I made to myself that I would really like to keep."

"If you'd have asked me I could have told you that promises are dangerous, even to yourself." Arrow told him somberly.

"I want to go home to Port."

"Why do you keep saying that?"

"You know... I think I might be homesick. All my life I moved around and never got settled then you brought me there and in those few months it became my home, but the real reason is Blade."

"I know you said you wanted to bond with her but do you love her?"

"Very much, she's pretty fond of you actually. Do you know why?"

"We go back a few years, does she like you too?" he shrugged. "You don't know but you want to get back?"

"Good point,"

"I'll take you back but I'm not staying anymore. I can't." Flint nodded his understanding.

"Do you miss Steel?"

Arrow thought carefully before answering, "I miss my old friend very much."

"Well, if I was to decode that I would start with 'old friend'"

"Just let it be Flint."

"No, tell me about it please?"

"He betrayed my trust before he kissed me and I'm not ready to talk about it."

"Steel's in love with you." She froze as if it was a complete shock, "I'm not outing him am I?"

"His feelings, positive or contrary, are never discussed. He's always been a closed book with a blank cover and honestly I don't want to continue discussing this." Arrow stood, walking to the other window. Thinking of all the times Steel had shown his feelings for her in a different way than she ever had before. "I'll still take you there if you want me to."

"Are you angry with me?"

"No...I'm more frustrated with myself than you."

"Let's go to sleep and start preparing to leave in the morning." She agreed and didn't talk anymore that night.

### Chapter 16

(Five days later and no signs of leaving)

He sat at the open window watching deer wind their way down the abandoned city streets. The 'night stalker' as they named him, seemed never to hunt or be around at all in daylight hours and it made Flint wonder why Arrow was so afraid of him. She'd started screaming in the night until she stopped sleeping more than an hour at a time all at once. He knew she'd seen the searcher before even if the words weren't rolling off her tongue. He made Arrow nervous, he made her timid and constantly second guessing every move.

"Did you rest?" he shook his head but stayed focused on the six point buck he'd spied out. "Me either, it's too bright."

"I should get you some curtains for that big window."

"That would only make my room stand out more from a distance."

"So I can box it up first." he smirked when she reached out to fluff his hair. "We've got tons of game out here."

"Go get one."

"Really?" he jumped up to his feet, the excitement bursting without control.

"Yes, pick any one you like." she passed him the stone tipped javelin she made as they traveled and he ran down the stairs, eager to do something outside.

Flint set his sights on a small doe without any female deer tending it. He was taking a cleansing breath when a flock of black birds went up in a riot of wings. The three young boys bound through the standing water along the curbs, laughing as they chased the deer away. He couldn't let himself get too mad but he was disappointed by the empty rumble in his stomach. In twenty minutes the deer would be back and he was sure to hit one but it felt like a smarter move to follow the kids.

Along the edges of the buildings he slunk as they ran and played without a care. He wanted to know where they lived, if there were others who lived around there. He was watching them kick a rock when the lights went out and he couldn't remember anything else...

When she looked down onto the roads and saw how dark it was, his absence was all she really noticed. Two days had passed since she suggested he hunt and there hadn't been one hint he was anywhere close-by since. The 'night stalker' was only three buildings away now and had killed the two old people before burning down their house. It wouldn't be long before she had to run or hide from him.

~~

Blade and Steel made their way up the coast in long, drawn out marches through the day and slept anywhere they found once they were tired. She never complained for a second and always made sure Steel was just as ready to stop as she was each time they did. "Hey Steel?" she asked one night after a very long uphill day.

"Yeah?"

"Do you miss Port?"

"Not at all actually."

"Me either, does that make you feel guilty?"

"A little, I suppose. Why do you ask?"

"I thought once I got out here I would want to go back. To work with my hands and watch that place grow but the closer we get to Flint and Arrow the less I miss it."

"I bet that would really upset Pine but me on the other hand don't care much."

"Why?"

"I've never really had a home so I don't get attached to places." Blade nodded, completely understanding how it could be hard for him. She'd never been adopted either, never had a family outside of the other orphans and the lovely staff of Westridge.

"Where's your partner pretty boy?" The woman at his side asked for a third time but he resisted. "I will find him and then you'll get to watch me torture answers out of him."

"I'll take that risk." he watched her peek out of the blinds, to check the kids, he guessed, "I wasn't trying to hurt your boys. I was only following to see where they lived."

"Much better," she rolled her eyes.

"They scared the deer away."

"Where is your partner?"

"She's at home, worrying about the crazy man burning down all the buildings at night."

"Wait, that's not your partner?"

"I don't know him." she sighed before leaning over to cut the rope she'd used to secure him to the chair. She wrapped what was left of it up in a tight coil and hung it on a hook on the wall. "Can I go?"

"Yeah, don't come back here again or I'll shoot you instead of questioning you."

"My friend and I could help you. We know a safe place."

"Oh yeah, why aren't you there then?"

He raised his hands, "I would be if she would have stayed but I owe her my life." The woman thought about it for a few minutes before answering him.

"Don't be a stranger then if you stick around," her attitude adjusted towards him suddenly.

He circled the block once to try and lose anyone who followed him. He was feeling shaken up but if he waited longer to get back to her, she might be gone. The door was secured as it had been since they found the place. The only entrance was from a loose window on the side.

Arrow stood on the third floor landing looking terrified, "Are you okay?" he shook his head, "Do we have to leave?" He nodded his head slowly. "Say something to me."

"I met someone out there."

"Oh?"

"A mother of three young boys."

"We need to take them with us." She stated without him questioning.

"Wait,"

"What's wrong?"

"You didn't tell me what happened to the old people." he noticed the shiver creep up her spine, "he killed them?"

"Then burned their little house down," Flint's arm wrapped around her shoulder trying to protect her from what she'd seen. "We should leave now, the family should come with us." She pulled away to look at him, "Only them."

"She's strong though, knocked me out with a rock and kept me prisoner. She thought I was with the 'night stalker'."

"Do they want to leave though?"

"I think they have to, that guy is crazy." Upstairs they packed their bags again in silence, he filled his own with cans of food.

"The converter won't fit in my pack. Can you take it?" She let him slip it from her hand.

"I should have asked her name or one of the boys," he stuck the converter into the outside pocket of his bag before slinging it over his shoulder. "What if she won't let us help?"

"Flint, she'll decide what's best for them once she knows her options. I bet she'll thank you."

"Yeah, let's go." They were almost at the bottom of the stairs when Arrow noticed a young boy running through the streets outside from the high window.

"Flint, look," she pointed as he disappeared behind a building and the searcher came into view. "He's out in the day."

"Tell me you stole a gun before we left."

"I have the butterfly knife you gave me."

"All I've got is a chisel, the spear was gone when I woke up in her house."

"We can't fight that man by ourselves, we should try to get to her and team up if her sons are in danger."

"I think you should go to her and I'll help him by being a distraction." she started to argue when he disappeared down the stairs.

"Where is she?"

"The gray place on Main, run west," He was gone. Gathering her strength as best as she could, Arrow made it to the bottom where he'd left the door open to Main street. She looked around for them before running towards the west like he told her. The house was at least a mile from the building they'd called home for several months and it wasn't hidden at all.

Arrow could see someone inside, puttering around with her chores in the slanted light through the windows. She started to creep around when a strange thought occurred to her. It had been five years since she knocked on a door. With a sigh and a bit of nerves she tapped on the metal.

"Now Colt, I told you to stop knocking on that thing," her voice was controlled and confident as she came to the front of the house, ready to scold a child. "Who are you?"

"My name's Stone, my friend saw a man chasing one of your boys through the streets." The woman spun slamming the door and tearing around the side of the house to a storm cellar. She threw it open to rip out a long rifle and another hand held weapon she tossed at Arrow.

"I assume you're here to help." she turned without an answer and headed towards the city as fast as Arrow had come. With little thought Arrow tossed her pack into the storm cellar and followed with as much speed as she could summon after the mad mother. She could already see Flint's distraction, their home was in flames from pavement to roof. It physically hurt to watch it burn and she could barely keep running. The woman she was following was a full block ahead, stalking the huge murderous man from the shadows of plumes of smoke. The young boy she'd seen ran out of the building across the street and grabbed Arrow by the hand.

"Come with me, that guy went this way?"

"Which guy?"

"The nice one, your friend," He led her down an overgrown alley and around the building where she saw Flint starting another fire.

"Your mother is going after the big guy," the boy laughed. "Why's that funny?"

"He knocked him out," the boy pointed at Flint and left her standing there in the road. Flint was in a rhythm of motions but she was stuck there watching as he threw burning bottles through windows with the young boy lighting them.

"Colt, what are you doing?"

"The city has to go Momma, help us."

"What on Earth are you talking about, put that down right this moment." he tossed the burning torch into a bakery window. "These people don't know what they just started."

"We didn't start anything, he was chasing your son and she," he pointed at Arrow, "saw him kill two old people while you had me in your basement."

"HE KILLED THEM?" Arrow nodded at the screamed question.

"Then he burned it to the ground." she continued.

"So he's not stopping with the food, he'll take lives too." the words were for her. "Colt, get your brothers and the rest of the guns. It's time to go." he ran off without another word.

"Are you coming with us?"

"I guess I don't have much else to choose from. Once they get back we should be almost done." The three of them burned as many of the larger buildings as possible. Breaking out windows and taking away as many hiding places as they possibly could. Flint sat on the curb watching the city burn and Arrow looked back at the home they'd kept for a while. She'd miss the safety, the vantage point and not feeling like she had to answer to anyone. Colt returned a few minutes later with his two brothers, all of them armed as well as she imagined military men did in foreign countries. "I got your bag too ma'am." he held the beaten up pack at the ends of his fingers.

"Thank you." he nodded and turned to his mother.

"Can we head to the stream first to fill these bottles?" His mother agreed and led them there before turning control over to Arrow.

"I think we should move all day as quickly as we can through the trees and see how far that takes us hopefully we'll be safe."

Chapter 17

She led the pack of six through dense brush while they still tried to stay quiet and shake the 'night stalker' if he was following anymore.

"Arrow, the kids are tired," she stopped and considered for a moment.

"We have to go another mile or two."

"I'll carry him," their mom scooped the youngest up and nudged the middle boy forward.

"I can carry Siege." The oldest brother said.

"I'm fine," he trudged to Arrow's side and they went on through the low grass and tightly growing trees. When she found a place that felt safe she nodded to the middle boy who sat down immediately on the grass. His two brothers followed suit near him and Arrow climbed the tallest tree to peer around looking for any sign they'd been followed but saw nothing. She was coming back when she heard the boys talking.

"These people move so fast and never drink, what's with them."

"He's pretty cool but she's so serious."

"Flint says that Stone isn't sure we can keep ahead of that guy because there are so many of us." Someone shushed them and she made her way slowly to the ground. Flint stood there with her.

"I'm pretty sure the boys are exhausted."

"They're also alive," she shrugged and he nodded.

"That too, but tomorrow can we pace ourselves a little more so they don't hate you?"

"Sure, I don't think he knows where we went anyway."

"That's good, you sleep first Miss Stone."

"Save it Flint, we're taking them back to Port so we should tell them the truth and get some truths from them too."

"Her name is Meadow, the oldest goes by Flame then its Siege and the little guy is Colt."

Arrow smiled, "You asked her?"

"No, Colt was chatting me up half the walk until Siege got to pouting and it all shut up like a dammed river."

"They're Port worthy." he smiled.

"How's everyone doing?" Flint stopped to give water while he checked morale. All but Arrow paused along with him. She climbed into a tree nearby to see the path behind them and searched for any signs that others roamed the woods. No one was in sight.

"Are we safe?" he asked when she got down.

"So far so good." She dusted her hands of the flaky bark.

"Here, have some water then we'll get going." She took the bottle and Flint moved on to Siege. The rest of the day Arrow hung towards the back of the group, covering their tracks and watching out for followers.

~~

Blade and Steel climbed into the low bows of the birch trees around them and waited for the sources of the voices they'd heard approaching them.

"Aren't you tired?" little Siege asked his oldest brother. Flint smiled as he came into view and Blade dropped to greet him without a second's thought. Steel kept put as they all grouped around his traveling companion. That's when he saw her, closing the distance cautiously and he slid down to speak to her quietly.

"Steel?" she half smiled, "What are you doing here?"

"Looking for you, is there someone else you were expecting?"

"No but I wasn't expecting anyone." he stayed a safe step away from her, afraid she would slap at him again.

"I'm here," She nodded as Flint came over to greet him.

"Followed us all this way?"

"We had to make sure you were safe," his eyes never left Arrow, "Couldn't sleep." She could see the circles under his eyes.

"Well, we're glad to have you with us. Meadow and her sons could really use some Port stories. I couldn't think of any." He agreed and walked with Flint to meet the four of them. Arrow just stood there staring, trying to figure out why it felt so good to see him, why she suddenly felt like she'd missed him. As the seven of them chatted and Arrow sat in the high branches of a pine tree, night came on quickly. Steel took first watch and Arrow stayed up with him.

"Why are you here?" she asked quietly when she was pretty sure the rest of their company were sleeping.

"Please, do me a favor and don't play dumb." his hand ached to touch hers.

"Fine, are you stupid?"

"I'm insane, right down to the definition."

"Obviously, do you still hate Bow even though he's dead?"

"I may always hate him but it was my fault not his." She nodded slowly. "I was jealous back then...Are you okay?" she nodded. "I'd actually like to talk about it."

"It wasn't easy to be by myself but Flint never meant for that," he'd heard Flint tell the story of when Meadow had him prisoner while they'd all caught up, "I saw things out there through that window."

"Like what?" his hand found hers, linking their fingers.

"Are there more of us?"

"I think we're mostly what's left aside from the well prepared and the resourceful."

"So we can't die, right?"

"We can but honestly why do you want to know?"

"I saw a man like us kill two elders then leave them strewn across their yard while he burned their house. He was tall and wide like you but he was angry."

"Like I used to be?"

"A very long time ago, we were kids." she squeezed his fingers.

"Arrow, is he following us?"

"I don't think so anymore." she glanced at him for a second, "How did you find us?"

"I was supposed to find you or else I wouldn't have. We just kept going until Blade found your mark." he copied it in the dirt at his feet.

"Oh, it was just a doodle out of habit I never thought you'd follow me."

"After I said all I did, I realized it was very badly timed and generally unwelcome."

"I loved Bow, he wasn't always thanking me for being alive the way you do."

"He thought you were invincible, even said you were probably immortal but he was talking to a drawing he'd done so I thought he was batty."

"I told him about me before you knew." he nodded as his thumb began to make slow circles on the back of her hand.

"Can you just say once that I mattered at all?"

"Steel?"

"You go on and on about how much he meant and that you loved him but he's gone. I'm right here, begging you to see me."

"I see you Steel. You mean a lot to me, I hate that you can't tell." she lifted their clasped hands. "I thought you needed me."

"History tells me we need each other but Port needs us more than that." He paused for a moment, "Is Flint ready to go home or did he agree for Blade?"

"Maybe she's a bigger factor than the safety but he wants both."

"I want to start first thing in the morning and we can't stop until we get there. We invited the camp men to patrol the Port and Shadow joined us then. He's different."

"He's fiery isn't he?"

"I feel like he was the entire camps level head and now they're sure to become hostile again if we don't do something to incorporate them."

"So you need me?"

"Didn't I just say that?" He lifted her hand to kiss it as Flint woke up. He crept his way over to them and sat next to Arrow, sandwiching her between them.

"See anything out there?"

"No," Steel answered even though they hadn't been looking well.

"You should turn in," he told Arrow rather than asking her.

"Sure," she stood up letting Steel's hand fall and going over to the hanging beds to rest.

"Leave her alone." Flint looked at him in a mixture of warning and anger.

"Why's that?" Steel was more amused than anything.

"She doesn't want the life you think she does or the relationship either. Arrow didn't even want it when he did."

"So here you are protecting her from her oldest friend?"

"I'm just saying to be patient and stop pushing her before she snaps and tries to hurt you or all of us again because she's scared."

"Are you sure who you're talking to here Flint?" Steel stood, straightening his pants.

"She's amazingly strong but her heart isn't as resilient as her body."

"Goodnight, keep a look out." Steel made his way over to the hanging hammocks and poked Arrow gently with his finger tip. She waited for him to be mostly on the bed before scooting to accommodate him.

"He's right you know?"

"You won't run away again because we belong together," They were back to back and she felt like he was finally beginning to respect her wishes.

Chapter 18

"We'll get going in an hour. It won't take long to get there."

"Should we leave sooner so it's daylight when we arrive?"

"I think we're okay," Flint nodded to Arrow's answer and stepped back outside of the ruined orphanage the core members used to live in.

Steel was outside helping the boys roll their sleeping bags up tightly to hide them in the building and Meadow was shaking the dirt out of their clothes after they finally stopped to have some lunch.

Steel had led the way the whole morning, keeping them close together and wary as they traveled the old roads.

"Is Shadow in Port all the time?" Arrow asked quietly once they'd begun moving again.

"He's been consistent, why?"

"From what I recall of basic training, he used to wander off all the time."

Steel shrugged, "Probably hiding his abilities because he thought he was the only one."

"Probably so," she fell back when the gates came into view and took Flint with her.

"I don't know what's going to come of me returning here but if I leave again I'll hide my notebooks for you and tell you where to find Tibur's."

"You'd let me write the story?"

"I think you'll lose interest once you hear the whole thing." He nodded and walked with her back into Port Harbor, feeling more at home than he ever had before.

Pine had already begun training sessions that included all the strongest people on Port. Steel joined them and taught the boys along with everyone else. He thought they could be a great asset, spending extra time to make sure they understood each lesson that was given and a little more than was taught too. He'd given them trapping lessons for two weeks before Pine included her first snares. Trigger even came inside to do demonstrations on survival and finding water, his men were on a constant patrol and Arrow was wondering if they'd get a break when the rains started. There was also a group working on fire safety and making hoses and trying to figure out containers for water. Arrow had been invited to watch them practice with the hoses and accepted since she knew the best path to the mountain stream.

"We really need a bucket system so we can pump water up the hoses and keep things safer." Steel decided after the hoses worked perfectly.

"Who could make them? What should they be made out of? We don't have access to plastics, all the 3D printing systems have died off and the little hand held machines that Willow made can't handle anything that big or that needs to be this seamless." Pine's realistic questions made them all pause for a moment until Steel spoke up.

"What about the water tank from the roof of Westridge? It's not small, we'd have to re-fit it but I think that's probably a good start."

"We could build it a ramp to slide down on. It's only three flights high." Crate was already planning the best way to get it down so Willow handed him a piece of paper and pencil to draw what he was imagining. Pine bent over his shoulder on the bark of the tree as he sketched out a ramp with pulleys at both ends to stabilize the tank while they lowered it.

"The rainy season is coming up. We should collect it and just use the pumps we have." Arrow looked up the mountain side as she said it and missed all the stupefied expressions before turning back to their nods. As they made their slow return from their adventure Arrow pulled Pine aside. "We should try to pull in all of Trigger's men and give them hot meals."

"Can you feed them all?" Pine worried.

"Give me a number and I'll make the food."

"I'll check with Trigger and set it up. Thank you for helping me be personable, I'm not the best host all the time." Arrow was surprised by the kindness in Pine's words. It had been a long time since they were friends.

"When the world's ending there's little time to be thoughtful but as we begin it again it wouldn't hurt anyone to be a little more thoughtful."

When the rain began they started to trudge into the mess hall, soaked and starving. Arrow had prepared a huge pot of stew and corn bread that took all day. She counted heads as best she could and there seemed to be at least a hundred of them once everyone had eaten. She pushed the dessert cart into the room and caught sight of Trigger who walked over to thank her.

"This was a perfect night for a good stew, did you do all of this yourself?"

"No, I've always got Crate there for the grunt work." He smiled brightly at her.

"He's a good man. I'm really glad we decided to stay around here. These are great people and it's nice to feel like we keep things civil for all of us."

"We appreciate you all as well. We should make this a regular occurrence, dinner inside in shifts so you can all put on some weight." Trigger laughed.

"Sure doesn't sound like a bad thing, not that we're starving." He picked up an orange slice from the tray, "Do you think you could make a cake?"

"It's been a very long time but I wouldn't mind trying." Arrow smiled and walked out of the dining room to put the rest of the kitchen back together for morning but Trigger followed her.

"You didn't ask me why I wanted a cake." She shook her head and kept cleaning the dishes she'd stacked into the sink earlier. "It's been five years since we all survived, don't you think we should celebrate?"

She stopped, set down the scrub brush on the edge of the basin and slowly turned to him. "No Trigger, I don't. To me it's like celebrating the day we realized everyone we loved was dead, the day we dusted their ashes out of our clothes and spit them out of our mouths and stumbled into this… half life."

"So you won't make a cake?" she turned back and continued her task, "I'll see you tomorrow night for dinner, sorry if I bugged you." Trigger had never been shut up in all his life, he'd never been deterred from continuing his own pursuits before but the cold and depressing vision she'd given him was enough to stop the toughest of men.

She was so angry that anyone would want to celebrate the destruction of their world. The thought was festering in her mind as she cleaned. Every inch of that kitchen was scrubbed and cleaned under. The counter tops shined and the floors gleamed as she closed the back door and wandered into the rain. That night Arrow looked for Steel after dark. He was sitting with Meadow's boys in the common room of the building they all shared, telling them a scary story about detonation from the underground and how the air was thick with dirt and you had to clear your throat ten times a day to keep your lungs open. They laughed thinking he was joking about the head lamps they'd hung on their bed ends to find their way around the seventy foot cave in the dark that it stayed all the time. She sat there until Meadow called them to bed.

"I need to talk to you."

"Should we go somewhere else?" she looked around and shook her head. No one was close enough to overhear them. She wrapped her arms around his neck, pretending to hug him as she whispered.

"Trigger suspects something about me, I just feel it. I think we should get out of here." He agreed, "Tomorrow morning, meet me and we'll head north." She stood up and walked to her room to pack up the few things she felt she needed to take along with her. Flint's knife he'd given her was slipped into a pocket, her clothes were shoved unceremoniously into the middle with the now faded photo of her and Bow.

Steel laid himself out on the floor in the common room, his bag had been packed for a month and all he needed from her was the go ahead. He'd always imagined going off with her into the sunset and being part of the stories that sounded too harrowing to be true. When they were growing up she spent most of her time getting into trouble for attention or helping others play pranks on their friends. She would tell these amazing stories she'd make up right in her head as the fifteen or twenty orphans listened with baited breath while the hero battled a dragon or his own fears to save the world. Steel couldn't help but hope that girl would show herself again on the road or that she'd feel comfortable enough to shed the fifty foot thick shell she'd built up in those years since detonation.

Arrow waited at the bottom of the quarry like they'd agreed and turned over stones, she heard him coming but kept her gaze on the rocks.

"Are we ready to go?"

"I want to go by the cabin then we can leave if you're sure you want to do this?"

"I can't be the leader forever Arrow and at some point Pine, Crate and Timber will follow us."

"Why," he eyed her over his shoulder

"I should think you'd see why they can't stay either," she didn't but she nodded as if she did, "They're like us, exactly and not the same as Flint."

"What's different about him?"'

"He's a bit of a hybrid, I realized that when he mentioned his siblings to me. They didn't make it through the blasts but he did."

"Neither did his parents, maybe we're just mutations."

"We are but it wasn't natural selection, aside from him if the story is true."

"When we get to the cabin you need to tell me what you know. I've been in the dark long enough."

"You don't need to know everything, you did once and it wasn't good for you."

"So I've forgotten it?"

He nodded as they entered the clearing around Bow's cabin that was little changed by the growth. "Get what you need and let's get going before Flint follows us."

"I don't want to know everything but you should fill me in."

"We should sit down." she narrowed her eyes but he shook his head, "on the porch." Once they sat and he was settled, Steel told her his story. "When I was a kid the government kept me in a seven by ten foot room and fed me gruel and tap water in tin cups. They did experiments on me and once I heard them compare me to someone that they were testing somewhere else and I started to shut down. If there were more people suffering like me I couldn't go on, being alone was all that held me together in the first place." he adjusted himself on the wooden stairs. "They said 'she' it was a girl."

"Did you break us out?"

"Arrow...they killed her in the testing and when they did the same experiment on me, I flat-lined." he sighed, "I woke up in a body bag in a dump and I found you cuddling a destroyed doll you found in the trash. We trusted one another instantly so I found us an orphanage and left you first with a note. Then I wandered in dirty and tired a few days later, that's how I know you."

"But I didn't know you when you got there."

"They tested on us for a long time, the memories are faded." he looked ashamed, "Let's get what you need?"

She stood up and went into the house ignoring the questions she still had. He'd known all about her and never said a word. She didn't remember the testing or the dump. In the back of Bow's cabin she knelt down to pull up the floor boards. A bag was set on top of the power supply, long unused and dusty. In the bag was her converter, photos of herself and Bow along with all of his letters and her original plans as they were supposed to be given to Bow when the Port was complete. As she zipped it up again she heard a voice.

"Put down the bag!" She dropped it to the floor, "Now stand up." She stood slowly and stayed facing away.

"Who are you?"

"You'll learn soon enough," He shoved her with the butt of the gun towards the door and walked her out where she saw Steel on the ground, surrounded by three armed men.

"What do you want?"

"Answers... Isn't the big guy supposed to be Port's leader?"

"He's escorting me to the north."

"Why's that? You seem capable enough." she gave a sarcastic shrug, pointing out the irony, "Don't blame us, we weren't on your radar."

"Anyone who may have taken advantage of us," Steel answered from the ground.

They dropped their weapons and helped Steel to his feet again. "Well my men don't like that you feel so violated, you're stealing from our leaders home." Steel's jaw dropped and Arrow stood stunned a moment.

"Tib led you?" was all she could get out.

"How do you know him?"

"She's Arrow." Steel informed them in a soft forceful voice as he dusted the grass and dirt from the front of his shirt.

"Then it's us who are mistaken, take whatever you need."

"Where are you all living out here?" Steel questioned.

"The mines and the quarry mostly, that's why we followed you here."

"Can we talk, what do you know?" Steel took her shoulder.

"They came to Port once but they were more into a nomadic life."

"We're doing alright in one place, we thought about returning."

"Silver would be glad to see you Wolf." Steel said to one of the men that had subdued him.

"Can we go then?" Arrow was getting anxious as she noticed how many men hid in the trees around them.

"You're both free to go. You'll be followed to the edge of the graveyard then on your own again." Their new leader said matter-of-factly.

Arrow went back into the cabin to get the bag, "We should be on our way then Steel and let these gentlemen get to Port if they want to."

"Slow down sweetheart!" Steel didn't see where it came from but he gritted his teeth.

"Look, Bow was my friend and I get that you were close to him but that's not okay." Arrow bit back the anger as best she could through her words.

Wolf stepped forward and apologized. "Silver told me about you, when we were friends as kids. She used to say you were one of the good ones, 'in a world full of people who surrounded themselves with mirrors Arrow carried a hammer'. It's one of the best explanations of a person I ever heard."

"Thank you, I don't know exactly what she meant but I'm sure it was complimentary. I wish we could stay longer but we really must be on our way."

"Where are you headed, if you don't mind my asking." the new leader requested.

"To send the rest of the world back to Port, you all should consider going there as well. It's only to a third capacity and growing all the time." Steel answered before Arrow could think of what she was doing. She hadn't spent a lot of time thinking where they would go or planning, she was just ready to leave again and Steel refused to let her go alone. She tried to see it as endearing but at the same time, she feared he'd become too attached.

"Well, I think I'll have our group get together and discuss it. Is there anything we can help the two of you with before you go?" Arrow thought for a moment then dug into the bag she'd pulled out of his cabin floor and slid out an old manila envelope.

"If you get yourselves to Port, please give this to my friend Flint. If you don't go then have someone take it to him and tell them you aren't hostile. It'll ease a lot of minds." It was met with a nod and Arrow turned to leave.

"We'll send someone, we promise." She nodded without turning around and continued on her way.

<u>Chapter 19</u>

Steel and Arrow had been running for half a mile towards the blazing buildings in the distance. She'd prepped both her weapons, one to stun and one to take down a man well enough that he wouldn't get back up. Steel had just run as fast as he could towards it, speeding up when they heard voices along with the crackling of wood and groan of heated metal.

"There's someone trapped in that building." Arrow looked at him with fear in her eyes, "I can get them out."

"No," she stopped running and grabbed his arm. "We can't survive fire."

He touched the side of her face softly, "Stay out here, I'll be right back." He turned and ran straight into the flickering flames blowing out of the building. She could hear the people inside and his crashing through locked doors and moving burning debris. Arrow had never been more afraid of anything in her life. She had no way of knowing what was happening inside of that slowly crumbling apartment home. It felt like an hour standing there with nothing but sound to send her imagination reeling until a couple of the people stumbled out coughing and falling to the ground. Arrow tended to them, telling them to pull off their shirts to take the smell of smoke away for a moment. Steel was the last out of the building his clothing tattered and burned, still smoking in places. He walked a few safe steps away to check his wounds, each scalding blister bubbling before dissipating under his skin again. If he'd been inside any longer he may have lost several layers, he wondered if that would heal the same.

Over the years he'd tested all kinds of different lacerations, contusions and abrasions to see what would happen or if they would heal but fire was not one he'd dared before. He believed Arrow was right that they could die in fire, a very slow, painful, boiling burn from the outside in kind of death. She came over to check on him after making sure everyone else was alright and far enough away from the collapsing facade.

"How bad is it?" she pulled away some of the fabric to see his skin was still red but mostly healed and closed up. "Are you okay?"

"I'm fine," Arrow stood on her tipped toes and barely kissed him, "and now I'm perfect." He smiled.

"I was so scared you wouldn't make it out." The building started to crumble behind them and Steel couldn't help but feel like he was lucky, for making it out of there and for having Arrow as his partner. He'd always dreamed of her saying she was worried about him or kissing him and now that she had it felt surreal. "What's wrong?"

"Arrow, I'm completely in love with you. I had no basis for comparison before now and I have to say, I've always and I mean always loved you."

"What brought this up?"

"I could have died in there, saving those people and all I kept thinking about was never seeing your face again. Never getting you really mad at me again to the point where you won't talk to me. Never spending the day with you and watching your mind work. It wasn't what I wanted to happen. It wasn't how I wanted things to be."

"Steel, are you okay?" He nodded, pulling her in close for a long, slow kiss.

"Never been better, let's check on them." He took her hand and started towards the huddling group of people.

A man stepped forward to talk to them. "Thank you so much, someone broke a jar of oil on the stairs and some of the other buildings were on fire nearby, we couldn't get down."

"I'm glad we were close enough to get to you."

"What's your name?"

"I'm Steel and this is Arrow. We're travelling around to help people find a safe place to live." The man took off his old and worn baseball cap and wrung it out as he looked at the ashen embers of the home they'd held for the past year.

"I suppose we can't stay here." He nearly chuckled.

"Doesn't seem very hospitable anymore, but we have been working on preventing just this type of thing where we come from." Arrow started to tell them about Port and where they could find it when Steel pulled her aside.

"Should we be telling them where to go or leading them there?"

"Should we really be going back for the third time? I can't keep doing this. You can either direct them on their way and come with me or lead them back but we can't do both."

He took his time answering though he knew what he wanted. "I think they would get in safer if they approached it from the east, we should tell them that."

"Good thinking." She went back and gave them detailed directions, names to ask for when they arrived as well as several provisions to help along their way. Then they helped the group of eight build a camp for the night that was quickly closing in. Steel built a fire and tried to hunt something down to eat but the collapsing of the buildings had scared everything away.

"Arrow and I will be leaving you all before morning light but if you follow her directions you'll get there safely before you know it."

"Thank you Steel. We had no idea there were any safe places, it's nice to hear that you're still letting people in." He nodded and walked back to the side of the fire where Arrow was sleeping.

"Is she your friend or…"

"She's Arrow, she doesn't belong to anyone or really anywhere. I'm just the muscle." The young lady who asked smiled at him.

"So you don't have a relationship to her?" Steel shook his head and looked back to watch her breathing in the flickering flames. "I asked because of how you stare at her, it's sort of possessive. The way a man looks at the woman he loves."

"I never said I didn't love her." He smirked at the nice girl who smiled again.

"It was nice to meet you both, thank you again." She shuffled back to the side of who he believed was her mother and lay down to sleep. Steel kept watch for a while then gently woke Arrow with a hand on her shoulder.

"We have to get going if we want to stay warm today." She roused and sat up, "It's sure to be a cold day."

"True and we gave them all of our water." She smiled clearing her eyes with the palms of her hands.

"I'm sorry I suggested going back yesterday. I know you don't want to live in the past anymore and I respect that." He helped her up after standing himself. "I feel like you'll want to settle some day and I'll be fine anywhere I'm needed."

"Really, it's okay. I think I get too sensitive about it because every time I escape Westridge and my past, I'm dragged back kicking and screaming or in tears."

"Never again," she looked at him with her half rolled sleeping bag in her arms. "I'll never make you go back there. I'll never suggest we should or ask when we are. This is your journey and I'm just along for the sights."

She shook her head, "It's yours too."

That day they walked thirty miles, he reminded her of some of the wonderful things about Westridge and Port. Things that weren't there to go back for anymore, people that no longer lived, and places that were big holes in the ground now. It was nice to think of it the way it used to be. "Do you remember when you were six and the old chef moved away?"

"Only vaguely, she was so nice to me I was sad to see her go. I remember madam Harvest was so angry with me for crying I wasn't allowed dinner, but you snuck me up one of those cheese fritters."

"You didn't even eat it."

"I wasn't going to eat anything Chef hadn't made herself. Until the new chef made macaroni and cheese, I can't resist that stuff."

Steel stepped onto a long smooth rock that felt cool to the touch. "We should stop here for the night, there was a stream down this hill maybe I can catch a fish or two."

"I'm not very hungry."

"Me either actually." He sat at the edge of the large stone to watch the sun set.

"Where do you think we are?" he shrugged. "I was thinking it must be Illinois or Michigan. I mean it's only September and we've already seen snow."

"Maybe we're in Canada."

"Maybe," she sat down next to him and laid her head on his shoulder.

"Mind if I put my arm around you?" she shook her head and cuddled in close when his arm came up. "We'd probably be warmer if we slept on the ground."

"We'll be fine." She sounded drowsy and comfortable.

"Have you ever tested yourself with ice?"

"No," she admitted with a yawn. He scooped her up into his arms and placed her on the ground before grabbing their packs and unrolling the sleeping bags to zip them together.

"This should be warm enough for us but I'm thinking we should carry more cover if we plan on staying in the open." She didn't say anything and Steel wondered if she was sleeping already. It had been a long, frigid day as well as windy while they travelled along the sheer face of the mountain. When he reached over to check on her she felt cold to the touch. "Arrow," he shook her but she didn't wake. "Arrow?" he was beginning to panic and took a deep breath laid the sleeping bags over her and began building a fire to warm her up. His toes and fingertips burned in the bitter wind while his palms worked the stick into the well and slowly kindled a small flame that he built up quickly with dry leaves. He dragged the sleeping bag around the two of them and pulled her close to his body, rubbing her shoulders and arms to get her blood flowing better again. It was an hour before she opened her eyes, "Arrow?"

"What happened?" He kissed her forehead, hugging onto her tight.

"I don't know but I'm so glad you're awake."

"I was just so cold." She tucked her fingers into her pockets and let out a breath that was cool enough it didn't make the cloud he'd been watching his own produce.

"How do you feel now?"

"Better, thank you." He shook his head.

"What else would I have done? Left you?" she laughed weakly. "We've both had scares now haven't we?"

"I guess so."

"We should get some sleep, can we stay like this?" she nodded, snuggling in and letting out a sigh. "Goodnight Arrow."

"Goodnight." He didn't sleep at all that night, checking her pulse and feeling her every breath to make sure she was alright.

<u>Chapter 20</u>

Within a week they stumbled upon a cottage, half buried in snow. The two of them dug out the front door and found it unlocked, inside the floors were covered in soft rugs and homemade furniture. There were quilts on the bed and thick coats in the one closet they found between the two rooms of the small home. A fire stove stood in the kitchen that was set up to heat the place as well as cook on. They decided to settle there for a while until winters hardest months were over.

"I wonder how well traps would work out here." Steel sat at the back window, looking over the snow and fresh fox tracks.

"Well, if you wire them with the brush they should disappear into the snow. A little bit of food and we should be able to get something out there to bite."

"That's what we should do tomorrow then, hopefully before the snow starts so our tracks will be covered up." He watched her agree and went back to looking out the window. "You know, this is the first time I've ever had a home, I mean besides the orphanage all those years ago."

"You don't remember your life before the experiments at all?"

"Not one memory from before."

"I don't even remember being there myself. I recall a saline bag once in a while when I'm dreaming and long needles spouting clear liquid. They seem like normal things to be scared of."

"Did you ever scream in your dreams?"

"Not until Flint and I saw that man burning things down."

"I feel like I heard you, all the way from Port or I felt your fear. That's when I headed towards you."

"I was so surprised to see you, in the middle of nowhere, almost thought you could be the person from the streets back there." She dropped a splintered log into the stove and set it on fire with a long match. "I wonder how they're getting along back home."

"I bet Pine has everything running like clockwork," he turned to face her instead of the window. "Flint and Blade are planning their wedding and building their own little house outside of the walls. He stills wonders where you are all the time and bugs her with stories about the road he's told a hundred times."

"So?"

"I guess I was trying to figure out if I could make you home sick."

"You said it yourself, this is the first real home I've ever had aside from eight years with my parents." She closed the stove top and crossed the room towards him. "We're not ready to stop this journey, are you?"

He wrapped his arms around her, burying his face in her chest, "No, I could stay out here with you forever. Right here in this cabin."

"I don't think we'll stay here forever." She leaned back to look at his eyes and blacked out, the next thing she remembered was Steel holding her and saying her name over and over.

"Are you awake?" she didn't say anything and stayed very still in his arms, "There's something wrong with you Arrow."

"What's happening to me?"

"I don't know but we need to find someone to check you out." He wiped her hair out of her eyes with his pinky finger. "That's really scaring me."

"It's not my favorite thing either." They were on the floor by the window Steel had been looking out of. When she collapsed he'd lowered her to the ground and cradled her in his lap. "Help me up?" Instead of helping her to her feet he slipped his arms under her knees and behind her neck and scooped her into his arms.

"Would you prefer the bed or the chair?"

"I just wanted to stand," he set her on her feet and stepped back.

"Are you sure you'll be okay there?"

"Yeah, I'm just planning on going to bed."

"Should have let me carry you there," he smirked as she shook her head. "I'll see you in the morning." She kissed his cheek and turned to get into the small bed. As she settled in her memory of their journey began coming back to her, all the long silent trudging and freezing temperatures. The days that they had to try and stay dry through torrential rain and the night they'd had to sleep in a lean-to they found on a mountain side. Their clothes hanging from the eves, flapped in the bitter wind and the sleeping bags soaked beneath them. The only thing she knew to do was cuddle in close, when the wind blew rain into her face Steel wiped the drops from her cheeks and kissed her. It wasn't like any other kiss he'd given her. His fingers twitched in her hair, his breath caught in his throat and his body began to heat up against her. Nothing had felt more natural to her then the slow way he progressed from there, indulging in his first touch of her back the first sight of her body and the first taste of her pale, soft skin.

Neither of them was cold anymore, the wind had no effect aside from drying their clothes and she wasn't thinking of putting them back on yet anyway. His hand absently ran up and down her spine as her head settled on his chest in the dark of their ineffective shelter. He found the deep scar in her shoulder from a piece of red hot metal flying from the pile that Rage had burned all those years ago. They'd never spoken about it after that night nearly a month before.

Arrow rolled over to see where he was in the cabin, finding him in the kitchen with a kettle on the fire stove. "Have you ever considered being a father?" Her voice was hardly audible above the crack of burning wood and the wind and snow outside but she was sure he'd heard her when he stopped mid-movement. "Have you?"

"Never," He set the mug he'd been holding onto the natural wood countertop and hung his head without facing her, "Do you think that's what's wrong?"

"It's the best guess I have. I've never been sick before and suddenly a month after we're together I start to lose consciousness and feel weak and tired all the time."

"I'm sorry," she could hear the apprehension in his voice and stood out of bed to comfort him.

"I'm not," he looked up to her weak smile, "I'm kind of excited. We'll both have a family now."

He started to cheer up as he thought about a small version of the two of them running around. "What if she looked like you? What if we have a boy?"

"I guess you're changing your mind then?"

"I'm getting excited too, but I'm still very worried about you. I'd be happy to welcome a little us into the world if I wasn't so afraid of what might happen to you."

"What if nothing is happening and I'm just not eating enough or sleeping enough. It can't be healthy that all I eat is wild animals and vegetables when we can find them and sleep two hours a day."

"Arrow, you've been my entire life for as long as I can remember and I want you to be healthy…" he sat for a long time in silence, weighing his words as carefully as he possibly could. "You know where you can have a balanced diet. I know you don't want to do that."

"Will you take care of me on the way there? I don't know that I could travel so far now."

"I've always taken care of you when I could, I'll get you back there safely. So when the snow stops?"

"We'll leave and maybe never return." She completed his thought sounding sad for the change.

"What do you mean?"

"I had hopes of staying here forever."

Steel stumbled into their cabin home covered in snow, the winter had been harsher than either of them had anticipated and each journey he took out for food went further into the untamed wilderness they'd found. He shed the saturated clothes and hung them on the hall tree by the door, trying his best to be quiet as he found his way to the bed. It was two in the morning and Arrow was all wrapped in the blanket they usually shared so he grabbed the lap blanket from the chair on his way over to get warmed up. She'd heard him come in but stayed perfectly still since it was the first comfortable position she'd found in hours.

"Did you find anything?" she whispered as he curled himself around her.

"For once, I think I did." He cuddled her close and kissed her cheek.

"Well?"

He chuckled at her impatience, "It looks like a repair station for those old cruisers, I found a couple that seemed like they may have some parts that aren't completely rusted through."

"Do you think you can fix something like that?"

"I have absolutely no idea, but what can I hurt in trying?" she made a sound and he rolled her over in his arms to face him, "If it only takes me a few months to build an entire compound, I think I'm capable of fumbling around with some solar powered motorcycles."

"That also just happen to be fifty years old?" He kissed her forehead.

"How are you feeling today, any more fainting or collapses?"

"No, the last week has been pretty uneventful. I'm sick in the early morning by noon I've eaten and had some of the lavender tea you found for me, that helps." He rubbed her slightly round belly, "I felt a kick yesterday. Do you think it's too early for that?"

"No, it's been three months. I'm sure you'll feel all kinds of fun stuff soon." He smiled at her, "I bet this baby will be so beautiful."

"What makes you say that?"

"If it looks anything like you there's no way it couldn't be."

"You've already got me Steel. You can stop being such a suck up." She teased.

"Never, I'll always be working to win you."

"Let's get some sleep you flirt." He kissed her lips and let her roll back over so they could get comfortable together. He lay there the rest of the night, listening to her steady breathing and wondering how to put those vehicles back together. The next morning he'd leave for another day or two, he wanted to search the mountain side for anything he may have missed. She'd been slowly emptying the wood from the hatch she found around back and seemed to be getting to the bottom which was another reason Steel needed to finish his exploring and get back to taking care of her full time.

## Chapter 21

Arrow pulled the last two logs from the open hatch and noticed a piece of rope nailed to the floor, she set down the wood, curious she pulled it as hard as she could. After dislodging the entire thing from the false floor, set it aside to peer into the newly opened place. It looked like a room the same size as the cabin above, filled with old, dry books and completely outdated pieces of hardware. A rusted robot stood in the nearest corner and Arrow carefully lowered herself into the space watching it nervously. The titles of the books weren't visible on any of the bindings anymore and she wondered what each of them could be about and how they ended up in a boarded up basement. Dust was settled in a thick blanket over everything still Arrow took care not to get near the robot. Its aluminum body had a shine in spots despite all the patches of rust and layers of dust. She suspected it functioned though it was clearly powered down. She grabbed the topmost books dusting them as well as she could before reaching to pull herself back up and out of the dark. She slipped to the floor, her ankles swollen and painful suddenly, disappointed and irritated she sat there for a long time. At first she was just looking around until she decided to read a book, "The Mechanics Run the World." The entire story spoke about how programmers began to fix all the holes in the virtual web around the globe. It mapped out the holes in the grid where cameras couldn't go. Far north and south weren't gridded and only got spontaneous coverage by the ten remaining scientists who shortly ran out of funding and interest to submersion games. These behemoths tore reality away from people in amazingly unexpected ways. Every choice showing the outcome allowed people to see each cause and effect mapped out, soothing people with the loss of the unexpected. Meals were often standard to the game and quickly tubes replaced tables.

It all made Arrow uncomfortable. After closing the book she lifted herself feeling weak still she pulled the metal man towards the opening and climbed him to get out. She lay in the snow, exhausted and panting until she heard a beep. Staying as still as she could Arrow let her mind have all the focus on her ears, listening for any changes or foreign sounds. In thirty seconds she heard a second beep and turned towards the hatch she escaped. In the dark below she saw the panel of the robot coming to life. There were no words to express the terror in her mind when she screamed and passed out, her head lulling into the cavity. When she woke her body felt warm and comfortable before she opened her eyes. She was in her own bed, the stove roared with fire and she could smell something cooking. For a moment she was content to believe she'd died, waking in a familiar place seemed like a fine afterlife. The sound of metal on metal woke her up the rest of the way. Quickly she sat up to look over the cabin for the robot she was sure lurked around.

"Glad to see you awake ma'am, how are you feeling?" the voice was brass and tinsel, not threatening or scary like Arrow had imagined.

"Um, I feel alright. Thank you." She gathered the blanket around her body that she realized now, was naked. "Do you answer to a name or should I just call you robot?"

"My name is Roger, what shall I call you ma'am?"

"Arrow would be fine. Where are my clothes Roger?"

"As you were soaked through with freezing water, I carefully removed them to dry and placed you under blankets. I can retrieve them if you wish as I'm fairly certain they are dry."

"Yes please," he left through the side door and she could see him walking towards the back then out of sight. She wondered why he was down under the house and who may have left him for so long or why. She had a whole list of questions for him when he returned.

"Your clothes Arrow," he held them out on stiff arms, folded and clean smelling.

"Thanks," she dressed with her back to him, "Can I ask you some things?"

"I operate to serve." He replied in the emotionless voice.

"How long have you been here?" she asked after clothing herself.

"I could better answer that if I knew the year." She turned back to face him, his green robotic eyes fixed on her.

"Today is November nineteenth, twenty-two fifty five."

"I see," he walked over to tend the boiling pot. "I have been here two hundred years, eleven days. I hope you're hungry."

"Actually I'm not but thank you. Were you a programming robot or a repair model?"

"Neither, though I can do both, my function was mostly household tasks before virtual modulators were standard home equipment. You see, I was built to clean a home and feed those who occupy it as well as maintenance every working part. My model was scrapped in favor of small specialized units. The lovely people I lived with began to load new programs into my memory and let me help them develop all sorts of new and exciting little machines. Then the second set of people inherited me and taught me to program and access V-world. I didn't particularly care for the experience. There was little interaction."

Arrow sat on the bed, stunned by all this machine knew and had been through. "Who were the first people to live here?"

"Cal and Pharana were the first to live here while I was powered up, that was nearly a hundred years after I was delivered to the building."

"Could you tell me about them?"

"That would be a long story."

"Maybe just the important points, so I can understand how you helped them." She curled her legs and smiled, pleased to have someone to talk to while Steel was gone.

"Cal was a woodsman, preferred to be outside and hunting or setting traps as well as cleaning his kills. He was smart, well read, even brilliant but hated to think someone might use it if they found out what he knew. The cabin was full of books when he lived here, shelves lined all the walls and he slept in a hammock in the trees even in the dead of winter."

"With this place and you, he slept out there?" She pointed to the flurried snowflake outside the window.

"It was his preference."

"What about Pharana?"

"When she arrived there was a lot of building to do. She was a programmer transitioning to be with Cal, he didn't do well with all the changes but accepted it slowly when she pulled away from most of her duties."

"Does V-world still exist?"

"There was a shell the last I operated but as I received no update on my reboot I am unsure of its existence in the present."

"That's a shame," Arrow paused, wondering if her questions were bothering him or if he could be bothered. "Are there any questions that you have?"

"Only one, why did you collapse, are you sick?"

"I'm experiencing a very draining pregnancy," his eyes seemed to understand. "My mate, Steel, is trying to repair a couple of cycles to go home and possibly get it under control."

"It sounds like he could use my help."

"Perhaps he could but maybe you could stay to keep me company." He agreed, making her a bowl of the stew he'd been cooking.

"This is full of nutrients, eat and get a bit more rest then I will tell you more." She took the bowl from his cold hand, sniffing at it. "Would you like a list of ingredients?"

"No," she tested, "It's very good, thank you."

"Truly, it is my pleasure."

"I only have one more question before that, where do you sleep?"

"I will go back to the basement if you wish but I do not sleep."

"Stay please."

"Is the home warm enough for you?"

"Yes but conserve the wood a bit until Steel returns to chop more."

"That is a task I can complete."

"Tomorrow Roger, I'm very tired."

"Goodnight Miss Arrow."

"Goodnight," he moved back across the room and put the rest of the food into a large container to take outside to the snow. With the power disconnected the refrigerator was of little use but once Roger had washed the pot he stored it inside. Arrow finished her stew and went to sleep, her stomach more settled than it had been in days. In the morning she woke to the sound of the kettle boiling, smiling when she saw Roger scrubbing at his tarnished spots with a wire brush.

"I'll get that." She took it off the stove and poured a mug for tea.

"How are you feeling after a solid meal and some sleep?"

"Feels like I could have slept an awful lot longer."

"You talk in your sleep." It was a statement she'd never heard.

"Must be part of this experience," she gestured to her belly.

"Have you considered that it could be psychological and your body is just playing its part?"

"You mean there's no baby or I'm making myself sick?"

"The latter," she cradled her little bundle. "I checked you with the med-scan last night. The baby is healthy and growing fast."

"What about me?"

"Aside from the replication gene you're pretty normal."

"What's the origin of that gene?"

"I am not sure, my programs are not fully updated."

"Had you heard of genetic testing?"

"Yes, my knowledge is not extensive on the subject. Humanities cruelty against itself happens to be a complicated subject with overlapping timelines that often fool our linear pathways."

"What do you know about it?"

"My last installation included a news flash, I can quote it for you. 'All subjects of the adult invulnerability trials have perished, children will be chosen next as they have a better chance of accepting the serum. Only thirty will be chosen, to save your progeny give him to your government'."

"There were only thirty?" she thought it sounded better than what she imagined since Steel told her what he remembered.

"This news came to scary reactions from Cinder. They'd just celebrated the third birthday of their son."

"I couldn't imagine. Were you the only way they received messages?"

"Yes, the hallo boards had all ceased to function and the food porter was so outdated it could not pick up signals anymore."

"Pharana built all of those systems when she was here before."

"Yes, she could wire old things to new purposes without ever having dealt with the components before. Robots are not capable of that kind of complex thinking and she always amazed me."

"Both of the women who lived here sound very strong."

"Not unlike yourself Miss Arrow." He turned his body, "Have I gotten it all?"

"No," she smiled, "I'll help." After an hour of scrubbing, she ran hot water down his back to wash away the stuff that clung to the metal. They'd still need to shine him up but at least the rust was gone, leaving behind little scuffs from the steel wool.

"Had I been stored inside, instead of underneath, I may have been able to avoid this."

"Yes, but I never would have climbed you and rebooted your systems." She dried him with a towel, "Steel should be home tonight, late."

"Have you missed him?" Arrow wasn't sure, she had enjoyed Roger's company and learning the history he knew.

"I'll be glad he's here."

"Should I make something for the two of you to eat?"

"He'll be ready for sleep. I don't think I've seen him eat in a month or more."

"Ask him about it to settle your mind. I will be downstairs until morning to make your tea."

"Thank you again for all you're doing. I can't believe I was afraid of you."

"It is natural to fear the unknown. I am only glad you did not remain fearful." He bowed his head and exited, leaving her a bit sad. He'd been so easy to relate to and knowledgeable about so many of the questions she had.

## Chapter 22

Roger eased her morning sickness always making her tea as soon as she woke each day. She hoped Steel would be as comfortable as she had been in his company. Arrow pulled one of the books from 2060 telling the first half of the submersion experience in V-world and the ways such a complete immersion was possible. Tubes fed the person when they chose to eat, the chair kept their bodies active, in an inactive state. They had choices but so few chose to log out, sometimes for decades. Populations began to drop around the globe for nearly twenty years less than a thousand births were reported. The fact made her sad for the entire missed generation. It was late but she read on by the light of the stove, seeing where all the nuclear power repeater plants were placed made her recall the vision she had all that time ago. Seeing how everything was perfectly spaced, making devastation nearly a complete loss around the world and then she understood what caused this global cleansing.

"You're awake?" Steel pulled his snow laden clothes off.

"I can't sleep. I'm so excited to tell you what I've been doing while you were gone."

"Where'd you find that book?" he stepped out of his wet boots.

"I used the last of the wood in that little side door and there was a piece of rope that pulled open a big basement full of all kinds of books and equipment I've never seen." He nodded, digging out an old pair of sweat pants. "There's even a robot."

"Does it work?"

"Yes"

"I could really use some help with those hover cycles. As much as I hate to admit it, the mechanics of them is more complicated than I know how to handle."

"Roger can help, he's been programmed with many skills, earlier he chopped wood for me and made a delicious stew last night. He's really great company."

"I'm relieved that you weren't on your own while I was gone. Sorry about the wood, I didn't realize it was so low."

"Never would have found the basement or these books if you had and Roger would still be rusting and powered off under the house."

"Has he taken good care of you then?"

"Actually, he may have saved my life."

"Remind me to thank him," he lifted her from the chair walking towards their bed. "What happened?"

"I passed out again, this time just being scared. He protected me and he checked on the baby who is taking after his father." He set her down carefully and kissed her forehead before walking around to his side.

"I still hope for your looks."

In the early light Steel heard the knob of the side door turn, trying his best to stay still, he looked from his position to see a hand set the kettle over the stove. Five minutes later the same hand took it off before it boiled. Steel got up from the bed and watched for a moment as the robot made her tea.

"Good morning." Steel spoke since the machine hadn't taken notice of him.

"Good morning sir," Roger turned to face him, his lit green eyes seemed to smile.

"I'm assuming she told you I was coming."

"Yes sir but also that you are her mate and the father of the child she carries."

"Her mate, yeah,"

"She asks a great many questions." Steel smiled, "Have we met before?"

"I've never met a robot that I remember, do I look familiar?"

"Vaguely," he set the brewed mug aside, "How old are you?"

"You ask a lot of questions yourself Roger."

"I have never experienced this kind of uncertainty. My apologies if I've offended you."

"No, just confused," he chuckled. Arrow woke and sat up, still under the covers yawning. "Good morning."

"Morning Steel, Roger, glad to hear you getting along." She looked at Steel, "Can you bring me my tea?"

"Sure, yeah." He reached across the counter.

"It is still a bit hot Miss Arrow. I fear our conversation woke you earlier than usual."

"He's probably right," Steel set the mug on the table by the bed and sat with her.

"What are we talking about?"

"Well, your robot friend thinks I look familiar. That's new for me." Steel laughed

"Perhaps I am mistaken. My updates are thirty one years behind."

"Who does he look like Roger?" She reached for the mug but did not pick it up.

"I'm sure I am mistaken Miss Arrow."

"Never mind that, who?"

"Cinder's boy…"

"I'm an orphan buddy," Steel scoffed.

"As I said 'a mistake'." Roger excused himself to go back into the basement.

"Steel, what if it was you? Maybe Roger knew your mother."

"I never had a family Arrow and if I did they didn't care about me." Steel stormed out, swinging the door so hard that it tossed a terra cotta pot off of the landing. She didn't mean to hurt him and still wasn't sure what she'd said but as she watched through the window he slammed his hammer like fists into the trunk of a hundred year old tree, raining snow around him with each blow. Her stomach ached as the baby rolled under her ribs.

"Steel," she screamed as her head went foggy. He heard her between punches and ran into the cabin followed almost immediately by Roger. Both expected to find her on the floor but she stood in a thin pool of blood and looking sickly pale.

"Sir, please take her to the bed. I will use the med-scan." Steel swept her into his arms and took her carefully to the bed.

"Are you okay Arrow?" she was in tears clinging to him as she sobbed. Roger wasted no time powering up the scanner to look her over.

"You seem to be healing and the baby is okay for now. Your blood pressure is high though and I am worried that you have had too much to worry about."

"Roger?"

"Yes sir?"

"Can you deliver the baby?"

"I can."

"It's not ready," she cried.

"We have to find a way to stabilize you. I can't lose you, I just can't"

"Would you like to read the scanner Mr. Steel?" He shoved the metal man out of the way and saw just what Roger had said.

"Then what happened?"

"She is a genetic mutation, we cannot predict the outcomes."

"If I drag a couple of those cycles up here could you fix them here?" Steel's mind was racing trying to figure out how to get her back to Port where he had no promises they could help her either.

"I will do what I can but if my opinion is needed I do not advise her traveling."

"Can she make it though?"

"Predictions are not possible with the information I have. The genetic mutation makes it very difficult to make reliable calculations. I simply believe it is unwise."

"Can you leave this building?"

"I have no designated parameters in my design."

Steel turned his attention back to Arrow who had been silently witnessing their exchange. "We could take him with us to help with you and the baby."

"I don't want to leave," she said with a bit of shame.

"Are you sure? It's getting a little bit scary to see this all happening."

"What can they do?"

"I can analyze the blood in the kitchen to better diagnose your condition."

"Yes please Roger," she answered while Steel processed what was being said.

"Arrow…" she was looking waiting. "Are you sure you're willing to die over this?"

"As long as this baby makes it, I don't matter." He had a hard time hearing the words but already knew it was what she'd say.

"Perhaps you're not as bad as anticipated, after the first tests."

"What do you see?" Steel walked over to see what the screen said.

"The baby has your mutation and I've no doubt you will complete your gestational period."

"He's strong," Steel choked up turning from the screen.

"It's a boy?" Arrow's eyes were the size of saucers.

"You didn't want to know?" Roger checked with concern.

"I did want to… I had this real old book once that showed something called a sonogram photo of the baby in the woman's womb. Can you do that Roger?"

Steel smiled and turned the screen beside him to face her.

"I've been tracking his movements since you first collapsed and taking vitals decreasingly for four days since." In shades of green and grey, their little boy wriggled and flexed with his fingers against her back. Arrow was in awe of what her body was capable of.

"Is he supposed to be so complete?"

"At four months and six days." Steel added.

"By classic standards, no, he is developing much faster than an average human fetus."

"How much faster?" Arrow whispered.

"You will only carry him for a month more but he will be born fully functional, assuming he can hold out that long."

Steel's dark eyes shown with hope as she studied his chiseled face, "Steel?"

"Yes?"

"I have less than a month if all this equipment is accurate. Can you make a crib instead of fixing those cycles?"

"There is an older one under here but it will need a new mattress." Roger had so many treasures downstairs where he'd been stored for so long. "The last baby of this home used it before he was taken to the Nevada Trials."

"What?" Steel questioned the statement instantly.

"The Nevada Trials were an extended military testing program to strengthen post V.R. children after failed attempts on adults."

"Roger, tell Steel about Cinder."

Steel held up a hand to Roger, "Wait."

"Waiting,"

"You two want to tell me about the woman who Arrow believes is my mother?" Arrow nodded as Roger patiently waited. "Cancel the command, I don't care."

"If it was my mother, I would care."

"It's not though Arrow and she wasn't mine either."

"Steel?" he walked towards the door.

"I'll be back tomorrow." He snatched his coat from the rack and left before either of them had a chance to argue. Arrow walked over and shut the door after his slamming proved ineffective, she pulled the quilt off the back of the sofa and took it back to the bed with her. After shaping it like a lumpy person she turned back to Roger.

"Tell me about Cinder and her partner."

## Chapter 23

"Cinder was curious about everything, took this place nearly apart when they came here just before the crash. Janu noticed some electrical anomalies that led to them trying to get his parents out. When they returned nearly five years later she carried the little boy but Janu was not with her, or his parents. She informed me that he'd been captured and she wasn't allowed to see him."

"But you said they celebrated his birthday together."

"Yes he returned after the collapse, it was a full eighteen months after her and the baby."

"Is Steel that baby?"

"The two bear strong resemblance."

"So you won't tell me?"

"I simply cannot be sure," Roger went back towards the kitchen but Arrow wanted to know so much more."

"What's downstairs?"

"I would need to know what you mean."

"Other than the books, what's in the basement of this cabin?"

"There is equipment for a hallo board, digi-goggles, a crib, piles of blankets, a working robot motor to power the house and diaries kept by the women of this home."

"Is that all?"

"No, I omitted the collection of movies."

"What is a movie?"

"A recorded entertainment device that occasionally shows truth."

"Are there any V.R. movies?"

"There are several but they are also very old and I'm not sure that the movies will play."

"Why?"

"The discs are nearly a hundred years old."

"I'm confused." Roger sat on a stool near the kitchen and gestured for her to continue. "No one lived here those years aside from you."

"Not exactly, there was a second robot."

"Where is he now?"

"All that remains of Charlie is his motor. The story is too long to discuss."

"Alright," Arrow stood to stretch her legs, feeling the baby do the same. "What was Cinder's boy's name?"

"Archer."

Arrow's heart dropped into her stomach as she reached out to the headboard to steady herself. "You're positive that was his name?"

"My systems information is incorruptible."

In that moment her mind was a swirling vortex. Had he named her all those years ago or did he find it somehow? Did he know his own name? Where was the proof to any of this speculation she felt? Were there photos or movies of the family in the basement? "Show me."

"Excuse me?"

"Show me everything the family left behind."

"I will go collect it and bring it to you. I'm afraid you wouldn't make it out a second time."

"Yes please, get it." At his normal metered speed Roger exited out of the cabin and Arrow exhaled for a long time. She found herself anxious and jittery but she felt like she needed to know more than anything. She wanted to speak to Steel but first she needed the proof... Archer, she pondered the same questions she had before. It felt like hours before Roger returned with the box.

"This is all the materials that were left by Cinder and Janu." He set it down on the bed, stepping aside to let her get a good look. In the box she saw lots of little things one edge. She picked one up but set it down again when she noticed papers peeking out from below all the other little things. Letters, informational papers and a few legal documents were on top. As she dug through she found just what she'd hoped at the very bottom. The photo was torn at a corner and yellowed with time but still the image remained intact. A pretty woman in striped dress sat in the grass with a toddler wrapped around her hip. His legs were long and his eyes were as bright with hope and happiness as his mother.

"This is Archer?" she pointed and Roger nodded. "Cinder?" another nod was the only answer she received. Arrow studied the old photo, trying to age the small child into the man she knew.

"Do you have the same belief as I do now?" Roger asked quietly from behind her after a silence.

"I'm positive it's my partner." She turned the photo over in her hands revealing the date on the back; 2220. "The years sound right." She turned it again. "What happened to Cinder after Archer was taken away?"

"She got very sick. Her heart could not take losing him. Janu and Cinder would fight over her eating but he always lost. When she died he packed me away."

"Where's a photo of him?" Roger shook his head, "None?"

"No ma'am."

Just then Arrow had an idea. "Can you sketch him?"

"I can try but have never been taught the skill."

"Did he look like Steel?"

"In size, yes, but he looks like his mother."

"She's beautiful." Arrow mused as she continued to study the photo.

"Yes, she was very beautiful and did I mention kind?"

"It shows on her face." She set it down and thumbed through the letters. All of them were from Janu who was being held in a military lockdown facility dealing with his knowledge of the mathematical matrix. His words were mechanical until you read each closing; 'with all I am and all I have left, Janu.' "Was he kind?"

"Before Archer was taken away he was but after he became very cold, angry and distant. If he is still alive then he is surely still angry.

"Hope he doesn't come back."

"He may return all the time. The cabin has snow so often tracks are covered in hours."

"Should I be so afraid?"

"Perhaps you should."

She gave him a serious look, "Would you protect me from him?"

"For as long as I survived. He would probably shut me off again."

"Let's glue it shut."

"What?"

"We'll close the button so it can't be pressed easily."

"That sounds like a perfect idea."

## Chapter 24

Steel returned in the middle of the night, creeping to the bed as quietly as he could.

"You're the size of a grizzly and sneak like a headless chicken." She grumbled into the pillow.

"Ouch," he straightened up and stood there waiting for the anger to spill.

"Go to sleep, we need to talk tomorrow."

"With you or should I go to the chair?" she tossed back the blankets to let him in. He wrapped her up in his arm. "Am I in trouble?"

"Why? Feeling guilty?"

"Not until you called me a headless chicken. Now I'm not too sure that waiting for morning is the best way to have a goodnight's sleep." He rubbed her shoulder with the hand under his pillow.

"The sleep won't be any better once you know what I have to tell you."

"Can't you just not tell me, I would much prefer the sleep?"

"I don't think I should keep this to myself. We may be in danger."

"Then we'll hitch up Roger and leave."

"But I feel like we belong here. I wish I'd have travelled here before."

"You've swayed me," he rolled over and sat up, "what did you find?"

"Hold on," she got up from the bed and went over to a bookshelf under the window. She carried it against her chest and walked back. "Roger brought this up to me after you stormed out." She passed the tattered photo and stepped away.

"Who is this woman...What's her name?"

"Cinder," she closed her eyes.

"The boy looks like me." Another long silence followed. "Is Cinder my mother?"

"I have no doubt."

"This isn't the first time I've seen her face."

"No?"

"From dreams mostly, I'd see her crying on her knees while I moved away or standing in tall grass picking flowers."

"Maybe you remember her."

"Look how she loved me." Arrow nodded her head, "Guess this means I did have a family."

"You had a father as well. Roger didn't have a photo of him."

"Why did they give me up?"

"The choice wasn't given." Steel just stared at his lovely mother.

Steel had made a mattress for the crib and built a rocking chair that wobbled but made Arrow happy. Roger moved the sofa downstairs to make room and Arrow had mostly tried to stay rested as simpler tasks began to tire her quickly.

"I've got to collect wood or we'll be freezing tonight." He kissed her cheek and tucked her into her blanket.

"Hand me another book?" he smirked but picked one she hadn't read yet and handed it over.

"I hope this one is fiction, can't stand another rant about V.R." he shut the door behind him and Roger turned to bring her some water.

"Do I rant?"

"In my opinion they are educational diatribes."

"I'm awful," she held her head.

"You are simply thirsting for knowledge."

She sighed, "With the life I had, there's no surprise in that."

"Perhaps not," Roger smiled.

"I think I'll take my book outside for a while." She stood slowly and made her way to the door, as soon as she opened it she spotted a man coming through the dense part of the woods. "Who are you?"

Janu stepped onto the property, "The owner of this house young lady and who might you be?"

"That's none of your business." Janu looked the brazen, pregnant woman over. "Why are you here?"

"As I already told you, this is my house. A man always comes back to his home."

"Roger," she called him from inside, stepping out of his way as he walked out blocking Arrow from his view.

"Hey nuts and bolts, want to tell this woman to leave my house?"

"I'm sorry Janu but Arrow has been here for quite some time and moving her now would be ill advised."

"What exactly should I do?" he shrugged off the duffle bag he carried letting it thump heavily to the ground.

"You're welcome to the basement." She offered, still protected by Roger.

"I've been travelling for months and I want my bed… You go to the basement." Roger opened his mouth to argue just as Steel broke through the brush with his arms piled high with branches. The men's eyes met, Janu gawked for a moment before bursting into tears. Steel felt only confusion. "I must be seeing things." Janu rubbed his wet eyes, dry.

"Steel this is Janu and we have been living in his home."

"Sorry to be the bearer of bad news sir, but we're not leaving for a least a couple of weeks."

"No, keep the house. I'll sleep in the basement." Janu took a step and Arrow glanced at him again.

"Wait."

"Yes?"

"I've seen you before, burning down buildings and killing old people."

"Can't say I've ever killed anyone but I did bury a couple I found already dead in a home in the city."

"Why were you chasing those boys?"

"He stole my walking stick and I'd just found it. Was it you who knocked me out?" he eyed her suspiciously.

"A friend of mine did."

"Arrow, what is he talking about?"

She touched Roger and he stepped to the side, "You scared us and I'm sorry."

"No harm done." Janu shrugged.

Steel had been staring the whole while at this man, who moved like him, was nearly as tall as he was and had the very same nose. He was putting the pieces together as Janu bent to grab his duffel. "What were you looking for?"

"A child who grew up away from his family, it's been a long time." Steel looked at Arrow who had a question of her own.

"Did you find what you were looking for?"

"I believe so," he shifted the straps in his fist, his hands matching Steel's exactly.

"Are you sure?" Steel felt he needed a grand gesture before he could believe what he was thinking.

"There's no reason for me to be sure but yes I am."

"My name is Steel and this is my mate Arrow. She believes the man who left this home is my father...Is it true?" Janu nodded, fighting back tears a second time. "Come inside and warm up."

Arrow moved aside to let them walk into the cabin, "Roger...Should I be worried?"

"I will not leave your side."